The Ghost of Billy Masterson
and
Other Thousand Islands Tales

Thomas Pullyblank

Square Circle Press
Schenectady, New York

**The Ghost of Billy Masterson
and Other Thousand Islands Tales**

Published by
Square Circle Press LLC
PO Box 913
Schenectady, NY 12305
www.squarecirclepress.com

First paperback edition 2014.
Printed and bound in the United States of America on acid-free, durable paper.
ISBN-13: 978-0-9856926-6-7
ISBN-10: 0-9856926-6-9
Library of Congress Control Number: 2014956915

Publisher's Acknowledgments
Cover ©2014 by Square Circle Press. Cover design by Richard Vang.

Here where the airs are always pure,
And wave and earth and sky allure
And whisper, "Let the best endure,"
The wiser thoughts and instincts grow,
Hearts truer feel and surer know,
And kindle to a tenderer glow.

Saint Lawrence River, here we rest,
And here we end our wandering quest
To reach the Islands of the Blest.
Where Nature's sweetest sweets abound,
And sacred waters, sacred ground—
The Earthly Paradise is found!

George C. Bragdon, "The Happy Islands"
in J.A. Haddock, *A Souvenir of the Thousand Islands*,
Alexandria Bay, 1896

Contents

The Ghost of Billy Masterson

(December 2001)

THE FIRST CHANGE BILLY MASTERSON NOTICED about himself was a sharpened sense of smell. It seemed to him that he could identify the odors of everything around him—seaweed and sand, granite and gneiss, sunfish droppings and eel skins. A moment later he caught a passing whiff of residual petroleum and traces of a long-gone Muskellunge.

His hearing, too, was more acute than it had been. He recognized the swish of a smallmouth bass and the flutter of a perch. Resonating at a much lower frequency, and exponentially louder, was the pervasive roar of the river's current. In the distance he heard the high-pitched crying of the girl—what was her name?—who had helped his friends put him into the water.

Other senses were dulled. He tasted nothing, nor breathed as he had once drawn breath. He did not feel cold, even though he knew it was the winter solstice and the river was close to freezing. Try as he might, he could not reach out and touch the large northern pike that rested only a foot or two away, like him just out of the current. Nor could he feel the sting to match the vague memory of hitting the water after his friends, along with Tom Flanagan and his girlfriend Mindy—that was her name!—dropped him from the deck of the American span of the Thousand Islands Bridge. How long had it been? Five minutes? An hour? Two or three? Time, it seemed, had lost its relevance.

Gone, too, was any relevance of whether he was

rightside up, upside down, or sideways. He felt a faint echo of awareness that he had entered the water feet-first, but as he started to understand what had happened to him, intuition said that his orientation no longer mattered.

Oddly, the appendages he once called hands and fingers offered simultaneous and contradictory sensations of numbness and a new-found keenness. He couldn't touch the pike —and with its sharp teeth bared he didn't necessarily want to—but he could maneuver around it without disturbing its rest. He moved through the water with no sense of propulsion from either arms or legs; when he moved the water did not stir. Yet he still had something resembling nerve endings, since he could feel the weight of the river pressing into him on all sides. Truth be told, he felt like he always imagined a jellyfish might feel.

Most strange were the several transformations in his sense of sight. Before, everything underwater had a greenish-grey tinge brought about by the water's absorption of other colors. Now, everything around him was tinted more towards the red end of the spectrum, with a hint of orange and, occasionally, yellow. He gazed upriver, in the direction of the pike, then turned to the northeast so quickly that he thought he saw, if only for a flash, in both directions at once. And was his vision ever keen! He looked up and saw through the surface of the water and into the air above it. He looked down and saw deep into the mud of the river floor. On either side, he saw the granite and gneiss of the channel walls ascending to the shore. Spatial distortion, which more than anything else made diving the river such an other-worldly experience, was negligible with his new, improved sense of sight.

He looked back upriver. Was that his body sinking down to the river floor, or was it just the underwater shadow of a cloud? What did he once look like, anyway? Tall and skinny? Short and stout? Billy Masterson seemed to be losing touch with even the basic facts of his old physical self.

He took comfort in the knowledge that the questions he asked no longer mattered, that the frailty of his body was now an irrelevant detail of his past.

"Eff it," he thought, appropriately enough given his new situation. "The lesser part of me's probably nothin' but fish food now."

Thus freed from the constraints of the living, Billy Masterson moved downriver. How fast was he going? Five knots? Ten? He could not gauge his speed accurately, just as he could no longer gauge time. Was the current making him go faster? He turned starboard into the shallower water of Swan Bay ("right" no longer felt useful in his new manifestation) and was quite astonished that he had slowed considerably, just by getting out of the flow. Was the current simply carrying him? "Port," he thought, and returned to the deep, swift waters of the channel. He concentrated as he approached the rushing water. He saw the water, saw the particles of sand and silt suspended in it. He felt himself being pulled in. He thought about slowing and slowed. The current, it seemed, was relevant only when he wanted it to be.

Where was he? With no way to measure how fast he was going or how much time had elapsed, he had no immediate knowledge of his exact location. Still, he'd lived on this river all his years and had died in its waters. He knew it like the back of the hand he once had. He called upon memory to get his bearings.

He knew he had entered the river from the bridge and was moving downriver. Therefore, Wellesley Island was to the port and the New York mainland was on his starboard. Based on what he saw when he looked either way, he was approaching Brown Bay on the island side and Saint Lawrence Park and Point Vivian on the mainland side. Ahead of him were several shoals, including Russell, Comfort and Pullman. He was moving along the American

Narrows, one of the most popular and dangerous sections of the river.

In his diving days he had visited several interesting sites here, including the large anchor in Brown Bay, the stepped cliffs of Cherry Island, the garbage dump at the same island's base and the steamship *Islander*, which was downriver from his present location, just off-shore from Alexandria Bay. But the one he had never seen, the one he never dared approach while flesh and blood, was the *Roy A. Jodrey*.

The Canadian freighter was bound for Detroit with 20,000 tons of iron ore when it scraped Pullman Shoal on the night of November 20, 1974. With the *Jodrey* listing to the starboard and its forward ballast tank breached, the captain decided to run the ship aground on the sandy shore of Wellesley Island near the Coast Guard station rather than risk more damage by continuing upriver. All 29 men aboard were safely removed from the boat before it started slipping down the slope into deeper water. Even on shore, the captain, crew and Coast Guard officers felt the rumble of all that steel and iron as the hull scraped past the sand and across the granite shelf of the channel wall. As it fell, the *Jodrey* severed the underwater electrical cables, causing a power outage at the Coast Guard station and at the homes of several year-round island residents.

Billy Masterson had not visited the *Roy A. Jodrey* for the simple reason that he was not stupid. He enjoyed diving, loved being underwater, especially with the fish, but he was a more-or-less autodidact diver who received certification from a friend in Alex Bay only because the friend owed him a favor. He had visited some of the other shipwrecks in this section of the river, the easy ones more appropriate for beginners and, with a partner, a few of the intermediate ones as well. The *Jodrey* was simply too difficult a dive for him to attempt. The current was fierce, as he now experienced. The ship itself had settled on rock ledges at several awkward angles and was filled with dangerous debris. The water was deep and very cold, even in the height of summer. The difficulty of the dive was borne out by tragedy: since the ship went down in November 1974 several well-experienced, professional divers had lost their lives trying to navigate their way around and through the wreck. Now, with the water cleared by Zebra mussels, diving the *Jodrey* was even more dangerous. As a friend of Billy's once put it, the clear water gives inexperienced divers a false sense of security because you are diving deep but you can still see. The clear water also revealed another danger—oil leaking from barrels in the *Jodrey's* hull, a leak evidenced by the rainbow swirls that often appeared on the surface just downriver from the wreck. The oil had not been removed precisely because of the difficulty of the dive. For all these reasons, the *Roy A. Jodrey* was officially off-limits.

Billy didn't have to worry about any of that now. He could handle the current. The cold water did not affect him. He was reasonably confident that he could navigate his way through the debris. He didn't have to worry about how much air was left in his tanks or whether he had the right mixture of gases for a deep-water dive. He didn't have to worry about when and where to make his decompression stops. Using neither the legs he once had nor the arms he could no longer feel, displacing no water, he did a little celebratory spin and said goodbye to the bends. He knew that the skin and muscle and bones that had once been him, with all their inherent limitations and frailties, were now no part of him at all.

Therefore, without aid of diving buoy or tether, he descended the almost vertical cliff. A small school of bass were clustered around a floating pool of oil about fifty feet down. Billy tried to shoo them away, but since he displaced no water there was no reason for the fish to take notice. He moved straight towards the oil patch. Only then did the bass sense his approach and scatter away from the poison.

Billy saw in the near distance the ship's bow,

wheelhouse and mast. The size of the freighter, a full 700 feet, was astounding. Before it sank it had been one of the most familiar and most impressive ships on the seaway, especially noted for its self-unloading mechanism made of a crane and a railroad track supported by thick steel cables and trellised railings. When Billy focused on seeing, he could view the entire length and height of the ship. Once painted black with bold red striping, now the *Jodrey* was corroded and encrusted with zebra mussel and periwinkle shells. To Billy's eyes, the shells glowed brown, pink and lavender in the ambient light from above.

He moved along the starboard side and explored the damage wrought by granite upon the steel hull. The hull was bent, its angle of repose adding to the overall danger of the wreck. He traced the gash where the steel walls were ripped open, first by hitting Pullman Shoal and later by sliding against the cliff down which Billy had just descended. Some of the edges were curled over. All of the edges were sharp and dangerous. As close to the steel as he could get, Billy saw deeper rips in the ballast chambers. He almost heard echoes of the ship scraping across the granite some twenty-seven years before.

He moved back up to the deck. The paint on the railings was a faded white where it peeked through the zebra mussel and periwinkle shells that had attached themselves to much of the surface. All over the deck Billy saw tangled railings and beams, wires and cables, stairways going up and down. He followed one stairway into the hull and found the engine room, where a school of sunfish sheltered. The floor was covered with silt two feet thick. He saw consoles, gauges and valves both large and small. He saw pipes sticking up from the silt. To get to the other exit he had to maneuver through a tangle of cables and wires, some still attached to their instruments, others swaying loosely in the current. He moved towards the stern and found the massive steel propeller shaft, coated in shells and grime like everything else. He ascended back up to the deck and down again outside the boat to find the equally massive propeller itself. He stared at the steel monstrosity, which had once given the freighter motion but was now as still and dead as every other part of the ship.

Billy returned to the bow along the port side. The name was still on the hull, faded but still visible. The anchor was also there, its angles softened by layers of shells, its curves elegant in the muted light of the deep. The hawse was still rolled up inside its compartment.

Billy directed his attention to the portholes. Most of them were cracked open, but a few still contained their glass. In one of the windows he saw two walleyes looking at him as if they were visitors in another element and he were the main attraction. One fish turned and swam into the darkness. The other, a two-footer, stayed put. Billy marveled at the walleye's color and pattern. It had spots of olive and gold, the gold deepened by the new reddish tint of Billy's sight. A series of dark saddles spread along the back of the fish and came to dominate the tail fin. The eyes of the walleye shone blue and green due to the layer of light-catching membrane that allowed them to navigate through deep, dark water. Billy wondered why he saw the blue and green now, why it wasn't tinted red like everything else.

Something about those eyes and the way the fish looked at him reminded Billy that there was another reason he loved being under the water. He couldn't place exactly what that reason was, but he sensed a hint of it. There was something out there, something he had seen but could not touch because, like the walleye, some barrier was in the way. There was something under the water that made him feel like that fish, beckoned onwards but frustrated by his inability to reach the other side. The walleye rolled a bit to its left. Billy saw its gills working as the fish looked right at him.

Billy had thought that seeing the *Roy A. Jodrey* would provide a sense of closure by fulfilling one of the important items on his bucket list. It was a good excursion, well worth his time, but he couldn't escape the feeling of incompleteness that the walleye behind the window was giving him. Billy needed to move on. He needed to find the object of his longing. He sent the walleye a telepathic farewell. The fish blinked.

Billy continued downriver towards Alexandria Bay, keeping the rock foundation of Wellesley Island to his port. How fast could he go with the current behind him? He thought "move" and moved. He thought "faster" and picked up speed. He repeated the thought and accelerated even more. He thought "up" then "down" then "up" again then "down, down, down." Having fun now, getting into a rhythm, he thought "up, up, up," counted to three, thought "down, down," counted to three, then "up" then "down, down." He broke the directional rhythm with a "faster" every now and again, then resumed the pattern he had established. He was flying now, moving faster than he ever had while swimming or diving or even while aboard Raphael Ostend's *Archangel*. If human eyes could have seen him, he would have looked something like a porpoise, rising and falling in the pattern of a sine curve.

"What if I were a porpoise?" Billy Masterson wondered. "Up, up, up, up, up," he thought, and felt himself coming furiously closer to the water's surface.

But it didn't work. He hit the water's surface as if it were frozen solid, two foot thick. He bounced back some distance into the deep. He didn't hurt—he had no body to be knocked back by the impact—but he did feel somewhat dazed and disoriented for a moment.

"What the eff was that all about?" he thought as he got his bearings.

More carefully now, Billy steadied his forward and upward movement as he approached Sunken Rock Island and the shoal of the same name. "Steady." "Slow." "Up." "Steady." At the same time he gauged the depth of the water—sixty feet, twenty, a steep cliff up to about five, three, two. He skimmed the surface of the water, pushed on it like poking the skin of a water balloon. Still, he could not move past it. "Reach" he thought, but could only reach so far. "Out," he thought. Nothing happened.

"Stuck here?" he asked, holding his place just under the surface. He began to appreciate the irony. "Exactly what I used to wish for when I was still on the other side. Part of me's glad I got it."

He turned to the northwest and moved into deeper water. He was in one of the most popular sections of the river now, where the shipping channel was tightly bound by a beautiful set of islands known as the Manhattan Group. Foremost among them was Heart Island, upon which George Boldt had built his famous castle. Billy had been in these waters at least a hundred times while he was alive. Sometimes he'd explored them while diving, most often while fishing aboard his father's old Hutchinson or in his own skiff. The alternating crests of islands and depths of channels combined with the weedy shallows of the shore made this section of the river a welcome habitat for all kinds of fish, including bass, pike, walleye, carp, eel and muskie. Moving around Heart Island, catching sight of the elongated shadow of Boldt Castle at the water's surface, Billy saw bass and perch by the dozens. There were walleye here, just as there had been back at the *Jodrey*, with spots and stripes just as beautiful as the one he'd communed with through the porthole.

As Billy crossed into the shallower water surrounding Harbor Island, he caught sight of a large pike, at least four feet long, laying in wait just like the one he'd seen near the bridge. The pike near the bridge had remained completely still with Billy only a couple of feet away. This one charged right at him, moving incredibly fast as if shot from a torpedo launcher. "Up!" Billy thought instinctively. Only later did he realize that "up" would not have been such a good idea had he been closer to the surface. He moved to a spot just below the surface as the fish blazed by him, its spots turned into stripes by the ferocious speed at which it moved. Billy followed the pike's movements easily enough from his vantage point. He saw the beast open its jaws and close them in an instant. He heard the crunch of bones as an unlucky perch became dinner. The pike chewed and swallowed. A moment later it struck again, this time nabbing a smallmouth bass that had wandered into its range of attack.

"Now there's somethin' you won't see from a boat," Billy thought, impressed.

He completed his round of Harbor Island and moved back across the channel to the Sunken Rock and Frontenac Shoals, feeling the current, watching the fish, loving every minute of it. In time he reached Cherry Island, where he saw the long, straight cliff leading up to the surface and the pile of garbage at the cliff's base. He moved closer to the dump and explored it, as he often had while diving. Maybe he would see something new with his improved vision. There were bottles, of course, also tables and wooden chairs, sofas and antique cooking stoves, refrigerators and even a reasonably intact Yamaha motorcycle.

Something caught Billy's eye as he approached a very deep section of the channel that extended down to two hundred feet and beyond. It was a glow in the water over near Stonycrest Island, a soft golden ribbon of light that seemed to emanate from very deep in the channel and snake its way up through the water. As Billy approached it he saw that it wasn't just a glow—it was a substance, a powder-like effusion that rose from a small crack in the granite and, astonishingly, rose straight upward, unaffected by the current. He immediately moved down towards the crack.

"I've seen this before," he thought, trying to recover the memory from earlier days. He rounded the small column of light. He noticed that he saw it clearly, as if it were in the atmosphere rather than under water. He placed himself in the column's path and felt the golden powder move around him—and through him. He felt electrified by the gold. Like a flash came the realization that there was somewhere else he had to be. He turned around, crossed the column of golden powder one last time, and proceeded to the southwest, back upriver.

As he approached Saint Lawrence Park he saw another island, much smaller than Wellesley, rising up from the river floor like a desert mesa. Its pink granite was bright in the low shafts of sunlight that cut through the water. The horizontal gashes he saw marking the rock could only mean one thing—that the island was cut by humans to widen the channel for seaway shipping. Billy Masterson still had a mental map of all he had known of the river, and he recalled that the island's name was Saint Helena.

"Saint Helena," he thought, refreshing the memory from not too long ago. "Also where that little French effer spent his exile, instead of here."

Billy Masterson paused, observing how the pink granite turned a faint purple by the occlusion of the water and the sediment that hung in it. He thought about what he had learned about Napoleon and the gold that the river people had named after him, the gold, he now knew, he had just encountered near Cherry and Stonycrest Islands. He recalled his own suspicions of what the gold was and where it had really come from. He returned to the channel. He knew where he had to go. He knew what he had to do. He knew why he was being called back upriver.

The water in the American Narrows was consistently deep for about two miles from here to the cluster of islands and shoals near Fineview. Billy repeated "faster, faster, faster" in his mind until he stopped accelerating. A nautical speedometer would have clocked him at 47 knots.

He guessed, correctly, that he was approaching Vanderbilt Island and Niagara Shoal. He slowed down. He passed

Frederick and Susan Islands and Mandolin Island to the port. He passed the Rock Island Light and the island beyond it, the one with the red house where Charlie Flanagan had crashed his boat. He paused for a moment remembering how he had jumped in the river that day to save Mary Flanagan, only to get her up out of the water too late, after she had already drowned. The memory still saddened him, as it always had while he was alive. Returning to his search, he noticed the Granite State Shoals and Castle Francis Island on his starboard. He slowed and went deeper, circling several underwater hills.

He saw two other significant shipwrecks there, neither of which he had explored before. First was the *A. E. Vickery*, a wooden schooner that had sunk near the Rock Island Reef in August 1889 while carrying 21,000 bushels of corn to a distillery in Prescott, Ontario. The *Vickery* rested at a sharp angle, with the bow on a rock ledge about 50 feet down and the stern resting on another at 110 feet. Billy saw the anchor chain as he descended along the starboard rail. The anchor itself had been removed long ago. If his memory was correct, it's the one on the front lawn of an Alexandria Bay restaurant.

The other wreck, right across the channel from the *Vickery*, was the *Oconto*. The wooden steamer had hit the Granite State Shoal on July 10, 1886, had broke in two, and now rested in 160 feet of cold, fast water. Billy remembered a few details about this particular wreck from the stories his friend Raphael Ostend had told him. The *Oconto* was bound for Cleveland with a cargo of luxury goods, including leather boots and shoes from Upstate New York tanneries and designer silk hats from the Ostend factory in Clinton Falls. The *Oconto* had sunk stern first, and had broke while divers were attempting to salvage the cargo, which was worth several hundred thousand dollars. A diver had almost died when the hull snapped and sank, but he barely escaped harm as the bow of the boat sank as well. Billy could not remember the details of how he survived.

Billy knew that both wrecks were just as interesting as the *Roy A. Jodrey*, perhaps even more so since these ones were wood instead of steel. He also knew he had other objectives to pursue, however, and would have to return later to give them a closer look. He took one last glance at the *Oconto's* upside-down stern, partly broken into a pile of timbers, and returned back to the waters near Wellesley Island.

He found what he was looking for in a cone of granite whose top was three feet below the water's surface—the underwater cave where Mary Flanagan's grandparents had first seen the golden powder that Napoleon had acquired in Egypt and had sent west in anticipation of his American exile. Napoleon never made it, of course, but the golden powder did. The river and its people had been transformed by it.

He had explored this place several times before. Back then his mobility was limited by having to wear his flippers, wetsuit, face mask and tank. Back then he could turn only slowly, more slowly if he got caught in the current or if he was holding a light. Back then the mask blocked his peripheral vision. Even after the zebra mussels had made the water clear as gin, he could only get an opaque view of the cave. To Billy, it was like looking through a camera on zoom setting—the object in view wasn't hazy so much as distorted by the refraction of light though the lens. And even when the water was clear as gin, there was always the danger of ruining the view by kicking up mud from the river floor.

Now, however, none of that applied. Now he saw the cave without obstruction. Now he moved around the granite as slowly or as swiftly as he wanted, always in a tight circle and always with the outcrop in view. Now, as he had already discovered back at the other end of the American

Narrows, the force of the current affected his movement only when he allowed it to.

Twice he dove to the base of the rock, with no worry about muddying the waters, and twice ascended back up to its peak. Forgetting that he no longer had the sense of touch, he floated just inches from the cave's entrance and tried to trace its border with a non-existent hand.

Billy Masterson got another idea, though, a better one. He slowly moved towards the entrance, cautious as he remembered the difficulty he had experienced trying to rise above the water's surface. The cave's mouth was small—previously, it would have been a tight squeeze without scuba gear. But in his new manifestation he slid through the entrance and into the cave easily.

"No scrapes," he thought. "No torn wetsuit, no dented air tank. I might be stuck here underwater, but I sure can get used to it."

Another difference between then and now immediately became evident. The entrance to the cave faced north, meaning that whatever late-afternoon sunlight there was coming from the low ecliptic did not reach it. Any other diver there on the winter solstice would have needed a strong lamp to see into the cave. Not so for the ghost of Billy Masterson. His view into the cave was like the view through a pair of night-vision goggles, with the significant difference that the scene before him was tinted red and gold rather than green.

"Is Napoleon's gold doing this?" Billy asked himself. At first he rejected the idea because none of the golden powder was visible. Could the small amount he had seen near Cherry Island have affected his sight like this? One thing was certain—the illumination was not external, it was inherent to his new way of viewing the world.

He moved further into the cave. The passage remained about the same diameter for seven or eight feet, then expanded into a chamber that an average sized adult could have easily stood up in, if he were able to squeeze through the opening and reach the cavern without an air tank. The cavern was all underwater, so Billy did not have to worry about negotiating the interface of river and air.

And the gold was here, although not in any chest that had crossed the water almost two centuries before. As at Cherry Island, the gold was venting up into the water, only here from a crack at the base of the cavern's far wall. Here, there was more of it flowing, a gallon or so per minute by Billy's estimation. He postulated that Mary Flanagan's grandparents, George Hibbard and Louise Dindeblanc, had seen this gold flowing from the cave's mouth and had assumed that Napoleon's chest of gold was inside the cave. If only they had seen it as he saw it now!

He moved into the path of the gold as he had at Cherry Island. He felt the electric shock of it again, but stronger, and a tingling sensation throughout his whole being. The water around him seemed transparent. The rock walls of the cavern seemed to glow.

And Billy sensed something else here, along with the gold. The feeling he had when he saw the walleye behind the porthole glass came back to him now. Only this time it was stronger, more immediate. Billy quickly turned around, thinking he might see a fish even more impressive than the walleye or the pike. Perhaps it's a muskie, he thought, or even one of the few remaining sturgeons. He saw nothing, though. He even completed a full-circle turn, just in case his new-found ability to see in more than one direction at once was an illusion.

The undines appeared when he turned back to the rupture in the rock from which the gold flowed. They were floating there in front of him, motionless yet undulating within themselves. They had the vague form of fish, although without fins or a tail. They had neither mouth nor gills. But they did have features that somewhat resembled faces. As Billy looked at them, first at one, then the other, then at a third, he was able to distinguish differences—wider eyes on one, narrower cheeks (if indeed that's what they were) on another. The third seemed almost obese, like a full-blown transparent puffer fish.

Two of them moved around Billy to fully encircle him. A moment after they stopped, Billy experienced a sensation he could only describe as a flash, followed by a brief time of blurred vision, followed by an even more perceptible ability to see in more than one direction at once—this time, in *three* directions at once. The tint and hue of what he saw had changed, too, from reddish to orange-ish, and brighter than it had been before.

"Damn," Billy said, feeling a smile even though he doubted he actually had the capability to make one. "This is more beautiful than I imagined." He saw that he had caught the attention of the undines. "You're all more beautiful than I imagined."

"Thank you," they said.

Billy Masterson jumped so high when he heard them answer that he instinctively looked up and simultaneously crouched down, afraid that hitting the granite roof of the cave would be even more bewildering than hitting the surface of the water had been.

"Do not worry," they said, speaking in harmony, almost musically, with one of them—the big one, Billy supposed—supplying a descant. "We have something to show you."

Billy heard a low humming sound which started in unison then unfolded into the same harmony. What he saw after a minute or two of humming took him by surprise. There he was, sitting with Tom Flanagan in front of a campfire on the shore outside Desmond and Georgia Snell's island cottage. The scene, which took place almost three months before, appeared to him like an underwater hologram. He and Tom and the campfire and the rocks of the shore undulated only slightly in the calm water of the cave.

Billy shook his head and smiled. "I live in a unheated shack over on Grindstone. I eat what I catch and grow. In the winter I caretake for several fine citizens who may or may not know I'm here. Do you think I found it?" Billy's expression mellowed and he laughed and waved an unlit cigarette. "I'm bullshittin' ya' Flanagan. I never got it out of the water, never called Geraldo Rivera to come up and open the chest, but I do believe I found it. And get this ..." he leaned closer and placed the cigarette in his mouth, then took it out again. "... I found it on the one and only dive I took with Ben Fries and without your father."

"How did that happen?" Tom asked.

"Because somehow Ben Fries knew exactly where to look." Billy lit the cigarette, his voice becoming serious again. "It happened like this. I went down myself that day and I could see everything. I mean everything. The day was perfect. Late afternoon. Mid August, 1982. The sun was shining deep into the water. I could see the weeds and the different colored layers of rock and the fish—my God, there were a lot of fish out that day. Big effers too!

"I was feelin' good, I don't know how to explain it. Keen, I guess, like after a good shave. I'd been in the water for ten, fifteen minutes when I saw this glow in the distance. At first I thought it was sunshine on some pink granite. I rolled over on my back and realized it couldn't be the sun because the glow was coming from the other side of a pretty steep drop off that was in shadow. Besides, it wasn't like a reflection. It was a glow. Like a bulb.

"I got closer and the glow got brighter. I could make out what looked to me like some banged up wood and metal around the glow, definitely an old ship. The glow got even brighter. I swam towards it, and got to about ten feet away." Billy paused and exhaled a large cloud of smoke. "When I got to about ten feet away a current hit me like a truck and turned me around, back towards the boat. It seemed like a current, but then again it didn't." He shook his head. "I *don't know, the more I think about it the stranger it becomes. The current, or whatever it was, hit me and I couldn't go on. I tried again and again, with the glow gettin' brighter and brighter. Shit, it was like it was cheerin' me on to reach it.*

"I couldn't do it anymore, Tom. My tank got empty. I ran out of gas. You know what's weird? When I stopped, the current stopped too. The water became calm, but I could not go on. I returned to the boat. I looked back once before I broke the surface and saw the glow dimmin' now behind me. It wasn't because I was swimmin' away from it or because my vision was blocked by the cliff or anything like that. It was like one of those fancy light dimmers the Snell's have. It shone bright, then dimmed. It was like it knew I was going away and faded. Like a curtain pulled over a sunny window. Or a smile fading from your face. That's the only way I can describe it. Like losing a smile ..."

The scene of the hologram shifted slightly. Billy and Tom were now looking up at the sky, where the *aurora borealis* danced.

"They say it's the river of Heaven," Billy said quietly, just above a whisper. "They also say the river up there sometimes overflows its banks and falls into our river down here."

As the northern lights cycled back through the spectrum again, Billy pointed up and said, "See that right there? That orangish yellowish color? That's exactly what Napoleon's gold looked like the day I saw it. I don't think it was real metal gold on that ship, Tom. I don't think it's real metal gold down there. I think it's some of that, some of Heaven's river up there. I bet Napoleon himself stole it and, who the hell knows, poured it into a bottle and sealed it shut. The French effer tried to become God, Tom. He tried to conquer heaven along with everything else he took." Billy paused. "You know what else?"

"What?" Tom Flanagan asked.

"That color? That gold? Every time I see it in the sky I want so effin' bad to see it again in the water."

The undines hummed again. The hologram slowly disappeared.

"Do you recall this conversation?" the undines asked.

"Of course I do."

"Do you recall the day in August of 1982 when you first saw the gold?"

"Like it was yesterday."

"What you wished for has come true, our friend." The undines' voices rang with joy. "You are no longer a spectator above the water."

"Was it you that day? Was it you who ran me over when I got too close to the gold?"

"It was not us, exactly. They were water beings, though, both alike and unlike us."

Billy tried to look where his hands once were. He saw nothing. "What about me? Am I one of you now?"

"No, you are not. Nor are we aware that such a transformation is possible, or even desirable. What has happened, as you probably already know from your earlier experiences in other parts of the river, is that, for you, the limitations of human living have been canceled. You are no longer dependent upon the lesser physical senses. You have been released from their hold over your understanding of the world around you." The undines moved, pirouetted. "Billy, you are free."

"I'm also dead, correct?"

"From the point of view of limited human sensibilities, yes, your body is dead."

"I became this transformed ... thing ... ghost ... when exactly? Back at Naguib Malqari's ship?" More memories came back.

"When you died at the stern of the *Ouroboros* you went to sleep. You awoke this afternoon when your body hit the

water after being dropped from the bridge. As you may discover, time is experienced quite differently in your current
manifestation than it was in your flesh and blood existence."
The undines paused. "Did you know that being dropped
from the Thousand Islands Bridge would … how shall we
put it … resurrect you?"

"No. It's just something I always wanted done to me
when I died. Don't know where I got the idea."

"We do."

"Oh." Billy's thoughts went back to his time near the
bridge. "Is my body still there?"

"It might be. It might also be buried in the mud below
the channel. Parts of it might also be in the digestive sys-
tems of various marine animals."

"Fish food," Billy said with a laugh. "So what should I
do now?"

"You have already experienced some of the transformations that you are capable of experiencing. These
transformations are caused by the gold. You have already
encountered the gold near what you call Cherry Island and
the gold here. Each source of gold can transform you in a
different way. Not even we are sure exactly how you will
turn out when your transformations are complete. Every
person's changes are different. We suggest that you search
out the other sources of gold and see what other transformations they cause."

"Where are the other sources?"

Before Billy finished asking the question he saw, again
in hologram form, a map of the river with the sources
clearly marked.

"I can get to them easy enough," Billy said. "What other
transformations are there? What can I become?"

"That is for you to discover. As undines, we already
possess many of the qualities that the gold can impart.
There are more that are beyond human capabilities and that
only we can appreciate." The undines moved closer. "Billy,

few humans have enjoyed the privilege you have received. Find the other sources of gold. Allow the gold to change you. Allow the gold to open up for you all the enchantments this river has to offer."

Billy Masterson was at once humbled, thrilled and motivated. The undines circled around him and he felt an electric charge through his whole being.

"Will I see you again?"

"Perhaps. We will not be in this place for long, as time used to be measured by you. We need to move on to other places, other times. We have many tasks to accomplish."

"Will I meet those other undines who tried to keep me away from the gold back in '82?"

"You may."

"Are they dangerous?"

"There are many beings in this river that you might not have even noticed in the past, but are indeed dangerous to you now. Be careful, Billy. If you need us, think of us. Think of us and we will come."

The undines to the side and behind Billy circled back and came to rest next to the third. Billy heard the humming again, saw everything around him go dark, and all of a sudden he was back near the entrance of the cave. He went through the opening and back out into the current. He set off towards the source of gold that first came to mind, the one near the Darlingside Palisades.

To get there Billy moved along the western end of Thousand Island Park and through the Narrows, a slim, deep passage of water between Wellesley Island and Murray Isle. He sped across the clear, shallow water of Eel Bay, delighting in the closeness of the ice sheen above him and the sand below. Soon he was in the deep, cold water of the Canadian Middle Channel. He effortlessly zigged and zagged around the many shoals that made this section of the river so dangerous to boaters.

By instinct he found the underwater waterfall on the

north side of Georgina Island, below the Canadian span of the Thousand Islands Bridge. He thought "stop" as he approached the ledge, then was carried straight down at incredible speed by the thousands of gallons of downward rushing water. He did a loop just before he hit the river floor, over a hundred feet below the surface, and sped upward against the current to the waterfall's crest. He dove down it again, falling even faster than he had the first time. "In-effing-credible!" he shouted in his mind. Billy repeated the ascent and fall again and again with an exhilarated abandon that did not leave him the least bit tired. He moved on with regret, but reassured with the knowledge that he could revisit the spot anytime he wanted.

Back in his fishing days he used to coast down the Raft Narrows in his boat, allowing the current to carry him and adjusting the rudder as needed to maintain a true course. He did the same now under the water. The river felt good and fresh, the waterfall in which he'd just played acting as a filter, cleansing the water of its impurities.

Billy closed his eyes—shut down his vision to be precise —and enjoyed this state of oneness with the river more than he had enjoyed any aspect of his new manifestation so far. He felt completely at peace, completely one with the water. It was a feeling he had yearned for often while alive. Now that he felt it, he also felt more alive than ever. As he moved along he felt a shock and a tingle, as he had at Cherry Island and at the cave offshore of Thousand Island Park. He knew he was approaching the Darlingside source of gold.

What he saw when he looked downriver astonished him. The gold was pouring out from beneath an angled granite shelf far below the river's surface. As it moved upward it spread outward and around to form a spiraling cone of glowing beauty. Billy thought back to something he had once read about conch shells and galaxies and hurricanes and a particular variety of broccoli, all of them characterized by the same pattern and measurable with the same mathematical formula. Did Napoleon's gold share that pattern? Billy was no mathematician, but what he saw was definitely a spiral, and, like a conch or a broccoli plant, was full of beauty and life.

Billy slowed and gingerly approached the inner cone of the spiral; perhaps, like a hurricane, it was also full of danger. He felt a shock again when he got to the center of the gold, only this time the shock was longer in duration and stronger than it had been before. The shock was so strong that Billy struggled to get out of the gold's pull. When he finally did so he felt dizzy, and the usual tingle was a degree or two more intense. He did not immediately notice any changes, however. The gold at this source was more powerful than any of the others he had visited, but how had it changed him? As the dizziness and tingle both left him he still felt no discernible changes.

Billy knew of three more sources. Two of them were upriver, one in the Admiralty Group and one between Wolfe and Carleton Islands. The third was downriver at the Brockville Narrows. Several reasons factored into Billy's decision to go upriver first. Going from Wolfe Island to the Brockville Narrows would take him through the entire Thousand Islands, a journey he had enjoyed several times in his previous life and one he yearned to enjoy in his new, improved manifestation. Billy also knew that the Brockville Narrows source, opened during the dredging of the seaway in the 1950's, was the strongest. He wanted to get the others under his proverbial belt before he encountered that one. Finally, Billy remembered quite clearly that it was on the way to the Brockville Narrows that he had jumped off Naguib Malqari's ship, the *Ouroboros*, in order to cut the cable that Walter Maitland's men had wrapped around the *Ouroboros'* propeller. He needed more time to decide whether he wanted to take the American Channel on his journey downriver and return to the place where he died, or take the Canadian Channel and avoid it.

So Billy moved upriver on the Canadian side, avoiding the waterfall this time by going around the south side of Georgina Island and through the Lost Channel. He sped through the Navy and Lake Fleet groups of islands without playing his zig-zag game among the shoals—this trip was all business. As he approached Leek Island in the Admiralty Group, he turned due north and easily found the source of gold off the eastern shore of Forsythe Island. It was a larger flow than he had seen at either American site, but nowhere near as large as the Darlingside source. Once through it, Billy moved south into the wide channel between Howe, Wolfe and Grindstone Islands. He turned straight upriver and back into American water around the eastern point of Wolfe Island, appreciating the linearity of the man-made channel, called the Wolfe Island Cut, just offshore of Quebec Head and Beauvais Point. He turned hard to the starboard and followed the shore of Wolfe Island until he found this source. He felt the tingle and shock at each location. Once again, he did not notice any immediate changes in his feelings or abilities.

Now it was decision time. Would he proceed downriver along the southern shores of Grindstone and Wellesley Islands, cut through the Summerland Group and then between Tar and Grenadier Islands to get to the Brockville Narrows? Or would he retrace his path back through the Admiralty, Navy and Lake Fleet Groups and under the Canadian span of the bridge? Would he, in essence, go American or Canadian?

He decided to let the river help him decide. He moved to deep water between Hickory and Grindstone Islands and stopped. "Which way you gonna pull me?" Billy asked Saint Lawrence. He found a deep patch of water that seemed to have no current at all and waited.

Some time later, Billy felt a slight wave of water pull him

south. "Don't be afraid," he told himself. "Just go where the river wants you to go." He also recalled the assurances of the undines near Thousand Island Park. They said he could call on them if needed and they would come. He wished he'd asked them for their names.

Billy let the water take him for several minutes before he was positive that he would return to the place of his death. Then he took off like a pike after food, charging downriver, accelerating to a speed faster than the current, dodging between shoals and in and out of shallow and deeper water. He was going so fast that he almost missed his destination. He was past the Summerland Group when he realized he'd better slow down, which he did with a noticeable swoosh of water in front of him.

His death had happened at the stern of a freighter. There were no obvious land or river marks to guide him to the spot. Nevertheless, he knew it, felt it, when he got there. He knew he was there because his whole being started to feel what he used to call light-headed. He stopped and descended to about twenty-five feet.

He heard the low humming sound. He heard the descant, although now it sounded like three voices or more above it instead of two. He slowly turned around until he saw the picture, undulating as the earlier scenes had back at the cave.

> *Billy climbed aboard the* Archangel. *He found the underwater welding torch stowed in the cabin, in a low cupboard. He turned on the gas and lit it. It worked. He ran out of the cabin and onto the wooden deck. He dove into the water and swam along the starboard side of the* Ouroboros *to the ship's stern. The cable was looped around the propeller three times. He steadied himself and examined it, figuring out exactly where to cut. From a lifetime of river experience, he already knew he had about two minutes to get the work done.*

One cut to the outer loop of cable took care of that. One to the twisted section beneath almost finished the job.

To access the rest of the tangled cable Billy had to wriggle in between the sections of steel he'd just cut. As he was doing so he was happy to see that they were drifting away from the propeller faster than he thought they would. He aimed the torch and cut. He was almost done with the third and final cut when he felt the pressure of steel cable snapping below him. He looked down and saw a piece of the cable coming at him like a whip. He returned to finish the third cut. His breath count was at one hundred five. He felt the steel brush past his legs first, then felt it hit his left temple hard. He let go of the torch. He stopped counting at one hundred twenty seven. The last thing he saw was the last of the steel cable moving away from the ship's propeller and down. Alongside it, also moving down, was the torch.

Billy remembered most of that as he watched it happen again before his eyes. What he did not recall, of course, was what happened next.

Five undines, including the three that Billy would later meet in the cave offshore from Thousand Islands Park, gathered in an oval around Billy and lifted him up to the river's surface. They seemed to sing as they did so, a slow dirge that nevertheless contained hints of celebration. They lifted him up and held him there. To anyone on the surface—in this case, to the group of French Canadian and Arab men aboard inflatable Zodiac boats who worked for Naguib Malqari and Walter Maitland, Billy Masterson's corpse seemed to be floating, which was quite unnatural so soon after death. The undines held him there. They let him go only when they were startled by the sudden splash into the water of Tom Flanagan, who had jumped off the deck of the Ouroboros in a failed attempt to save his drowned friend.

"Huh," Billy said thoughtfully when the show ended. "I've always wondered how that happened." He felt that talking would soothe his grief. He thought he was talking to his three new undine friends.

When he turned around, however, he encountered not the friendly faces of the water beings who had helped him earlier, but rather the many faces of a much larger group of undines—twelve? twenty? more?—undines that were noticeably hostile.

Billy thought back to what the friendly ones had said about the time Billy had been knocked away from Napoleon's gold. "They were both alike and unlike us," they had said. Now, with just a glance, Billy knew what they had meant.

"Were you the effers ..." he began to say. He stopped when he felt hit by a force many times harder than the one he'd been hit by the first time he saw the gold twenty years before on his excursion with his friend Ben Fries.

"Strange thing is," he said to himself, feeling a horrid psychic pain that was far more acute than anything he'd felt when alive, "I didn't even see them comin'."

The pain throughout his whole being got worse as he shot up towards the surface. He felt as if he were simultaneously exploding and being crushed in a metal compactor. Billy braced himself for what promised to be even more agony when he inevitably hit the surface and bounced back into the water, probably to face another thrashing.

He braced himself for impact. He mentally clenched the fists he didn't have and closed the eyes (or whatever they were) that were blinded by the pain. The last thing he expected was to be shot out of the water like a submarine-launched missile.

He was already fifty feet in the air when he realized he could still smell, still hear and, yes, still see. He smelled seaweed again and the sap of pine trees and ozone. He heard the slow wail of a loon and the high-pitched chirp of a fisher. He saw the black sky and the moon-illuminated clouds and the array of stars beyond. But he was slowing down, which meant that flying was not one of the attributes that the gold had given him. He was approaching the apex of his arc. He prepared himself for the fall.

When he looked down he was surprised to see a wooden steamship heading upriver, a ship Billy knew he had seen somewhere before. As he crested the apex and started his inevitable descent he tried to aim himself towards the port side of the steamer's bow. Forty feet, thirty, twenty, ten —his trajectory was so accurate that he had second thoughts about his inability to fly. Maybe it had just taken him a few minutes to get used to it. But he kept going down, even when he tried repeating "up!" He also started to recall the boat he was rapidly approaching. He didn't like the recollection one bit. He hoped he would find information to contradict the memory.

He saw the boat's name as he passed it. The word was painted in thick black stencil on the white hull, and Billy knew immediately that his night vision was just as keen as his underwater vision, even though he was at the end of an unplanned, violent journey through space and time.

"What the eff?" was all he could say as he crashed into the water. He had little time to consider an answer. His first priority was to avoid being hit by the *Oconto* as the ship, on its final voyage from Ogdensburg, passed over him just inches away.

Lady Ostend Meets

an Underwater Adventurer of Diverse

and Sundry Accomplishments

(July 1886)

LADY OSTEND, AT THE STERN, tried to maintain her composure as her husband rowed the skiff through the Narrows, a deep sliver of water between Wellesley Island on the left and Murray Isle on the right. She breathed deep, taking in the warm, wet air that blew from Lake Ontario to the west. She looked straight ahead and a little to the left, waiting to see what she had heard was there, wondering if the reality of the scene would match her imagination.

Michael's legs pressed hard against the seat between them. His arms strained underneath the sweat-soaked linen of his shirt. His head moved furiously, like the knob at the end of a pumpjack. Once through the Narrows, Michael pulled the left oar out of the water every other stroke to make the turn into wider water. A wash of spray splashed over the gunwale as the boat listed to the starboard. Michael straightened the skiff and rowed even harder. Thus occupied he did not see what Lady Ostend saw—the bow of the otherwise submerged steamship *Oconto* sticking up out of the water at a twenty-five to thirty degree angle.

Lady Ostend let out a gasp.

"That bad?" Michael asked, not turning around, not slowing down either.

"I've never seen anything like it," Lady Ostend said. "I never thought I *could* see anything like it."

Michael removed both oars from the water and let the skiff coast. He turned over his right shoulder, took in the scene with a glance, and resumed rowing.

"How big a ship is it? Do you remember?"

"One hundred and twenty feet from stern to bow," Lady Ostend answered.

"How much of it is out of the water, would you guess?"

"Twenty feet."

"And the rest of it under. The question is, where did they put the iron? If it's in the stern, and if the stern is already resting on rock, the boat might not sink any deeper."

"The other question is, how wide of a rock is the stern resting on?"

"So it is," Michael said.

A few minutes later, the Ostends were moored athwart the barge *Argosy*. George Hall, the stocky red-haired owner of the barge and of the tug that brought it to the scene of the wreck, offered Lady Ostend a hand to help her climb the rope ladder to the barge's deck. Dressed as she was in a light shift tucked into a pair of trousers, which were in turn tucked into a pair of long leather boots, she had little trouble pulling herself onto the rope ladder and from there onto the barge.

Once Michael Ostend had followed her aboard, George Hall gestured towards the bow of the wooden freighter, no more than ten feet away from where they stood. He explained that about four-fifths of the boat was under water. He estimated that the tear was about seventy to eighty feet back from the bow, forty to fifty feet up from the stern, on the port side of the hull. George Hall postulated that there could be a good deal of air still in the hold from that point up to the water line.

Lady Ostend understood. Her husband, holding her

hand, led her away from Captain Hall and sought consulta-
tion, as he always did on important business matters. Should
they try to salvage some of the cargo? Their goods alone,
three hundred silk top hats manufactured at the family's
Clinton Falls, New York, factory, were worth over one hundred thousand dollars. Yes, the hats were covered by
insurance, but it seemed to Michael quite a shame to allow
such fine workmanship go to waste.

Lady Ostend raised concerns about the human danger.
How big of a risk would it be to send in a team of divers to
extract the cargo? No one knew where on the ship the hats
had been stowed. How difficult would it be to dry off any
that were now underwater? One thing, at least, was certain
—nothing would happen until the insurance agents arrived
to assess the situation.

"What took you so long to get here?" George Hall
asked after giving them a moment's privacy.

"We weren't at home," Michael Ostend said. "We were
at the Davis' place on Murray Isle. We read the news in the
Herald and came here immediately."

George Hall looked behind him. "In a skiff?"

"More reliable than a launch," Michael said. George
Hall nodded in agreement. "Have the insurance people
come yet?" Michael asked.

"Sometime today. They're from Buffalo."

When the insurance adjusters arrived later that morning,
they insisted that a salvage operation must be attempted before they would even consider paying out a penny. With the
adjusters' approval given, George Hall jumped into action.
He had several divers on the barge and still others on the
shore, all of them at the ready. He had the contracts written
up. His price was ten percent of the value of all cargo that
his men reclaimed. Apparently, Hall had already bought the
Oconto itself from its owner, Anderson & Bates of Cleveland. It was obviously in his interest to get his men down
there as quickly as he could to retrieve whatever cargo and

equipment they could. The Ostends consulted again. They agreed that George Hall was both trustworthy and reliable. He was clearly the right man for the job.

Later, as George Hall checked his equipment and Michael Ostend discussed details with the insurance agent, one of Hall's divers joined Lady Ostend at the barge's railing. He was tall and thick with close-cropped black hair cut straight across his forehead. "My lady," he said as he approached.

"Just Lady, if you please," she said with a smile. "I wear it as a name rather than a title. The title, like taffeta and tulle, is best left in the ballroom."

"Mrs. Ostend, then, if it's all the same. My name is Joseph Jelly, ma'am. I'm one of the men going down to reclaim your hats. You can call me just Joe."

"Pleased to meet you, Mr. Jelly."

"Likewise." Joe Jelly said, pleased that she called him mister. He reached forward. His arms were so long that for a moment Lady Ostend thought he might be able to touch the *Oconto*. "This is the third vessel in two years the Granite Shoal has laid to rest," he said.

"The Saint Lawrence River has a mind of it's own," Lady Ostend said. "We are uninvited guests, with our steamship freighters and paddle-wheel yachts and naphtha-fired runabouts. Uninvited and sometimes unwanted."

"I can't blame it one bit for not wanting our loud and dirty boats, Mrs. Ostend. I'm impressed that your husband rowed over here in that skiff."

Lady Ostend turned to face him. "Are you old-fashioned, Mr. Jelly?"

He pointed to the *Oconto* and waved a hand at George Hall's barges and tug. "My memories of the river before all this came are the fondest memories of all," he said.

"All this provides you with a comfortable living."

"Indeed it does. And yet," Mr. Jelly hesitated before

completing the thought. "I mean no offense, Mrs. Ostend, but do you enjoy silk hats?"

Lady Ostend burst out laughing. "I see your point. I see it right away. The Ostends make hats, but we are so much more than haberdashers."

"I earn a living by salvaging wrecks from the river. But to me this river is so much more than a wrecker of ships. Compared to the river itself, the boats we build and float on its surface aren't very impressive, at least not to me. I might work on and off boats all day, ma'am, but I'm no worshiper of the machine." Joe Jelly paused for a long time while Lady Ostend enjoyed the smile that followed her laughter. "I do share one thing with the worshipers of the machine, though."

"Which is?" she asked.

"I don't trust it, this river. I respect it more than they do, but I don't trust it. This river's like life itself, Mrs. Ostend. I take that back. This river *is* life itself. Untamed, unpredictable and unforgiving."

She looked at him more seriously. "I would have understood you more clearly if you left it at the river providing you with a comfortable living, even with your dislike of machines."

"How old are you, Mrs. Ostend? If you don't mind me asking."

"Not at all. I'm twenty-three."

"Have you lived on the river all your life?"

"Yes. I was born and raised in Prescott. Michael and I moved to our family islands as soon as we married in 1884. Since then I've spent the past two summers there, with him."

"Yes, in your new castle. Valhalla, right? I've seen it, but only at a distance."

"You may yet have your chance to see it up close, Mr. Jelly. Michael and I are hosting a modest soiree at Valhalla sometime this autumn. Perhaps you can attend if you're not otherwise occupied in reclaiming wrecks from the river."

"I'm honored, ma'am." He gave a slight bow, which Lady Ostend didn't expect but certainly did appreciate.

"Do you have a tuxedo?" she asked.

"No."

"I'll be sure to have Michael take you to Kingston to buy one."

"Ma'am ..."

Lady Ostend dismissed his protest with her hand. "Nonsense, Mr. Jelly. The purpose of the Ostend Ball, as I'm calling it, is to bring together friends of the river for conversation about the river. This year's honored guest is Captain Doctor Smithson from Kingston, who is about to return from Egypt and assume the position of Chief Medical Officer at the Royal Military College. He knows a great deal about the Saint Lawrence. The two of you should get along quite well. If you cannot afford a tuxedo, I'll also be sure to have Michael pay for it."

"I appreciate your generosity, Mrs. Ostend. Thank you." Joseph Jelly was smiling, obviously elated at the impending and sudden improvement in his social life. He was also pensive, alternating glances from the top of the *Oconto's* bow to the dark water below it.

"You have something else to say?" Lady Ostend asked.

"Yes, getting back to what I was saying about the river. You've only been here—fully here, on the river—for two years, and then only during the summer. Have you ever been in it, Mrs. Ostend? Not just swimming, but really in it? Have you ever been *down there*, ma'am?"

She was looking down there now. The water was murky, greenish-brown to her eye. She had to admit that what attracted her to this place wasn't so much the river itself as the islands on it. A thousand lush emeralds studding a rather blasé strip of liquid leather, she thought. And her emeralds, her and Michael's, were the most dazzling and precious island-stones of all.

"I'll take your silence to mean you haven't," Joe Jelly continued. "Take it from me—it's a different world."

"How many times have you been down there?"

"Perhaps more than anyone," he answered in a solemn tone.

"Even more than Mr. Hall?"

"Yes. Besides, George Hall does indeed love the machines, especially his barges and tugs and cranes and winches. I think his appreciation of all that mechanical power blinds him from seeing what's really there. I don't think he knows how different our river really is."

Lady Ostend was listening carefully now. She had not been as deep in the river as Joe Jelly was describing. But she had *looked* deep into the river while on the shore of her emerald islands, and she had seen something in the water, had felt something tugging at her emotional and spiritual attention, especially on a cool day in the late spring before the algae grew and became thick. Was this what Joe Jelly was getting at? Or was he simply trying to describe a sturgeon that had once snuck up on him from behind a patch a seaweed?

"I'm not just talking about the fish," he said as if reading her mind. "I'm talking about something in the river that's like the water itself, only *alive*. And there's something else, Mrs. Ostend. George Hall says it's just the sunlight slicing through the sediment and playing with my eyes, but I know bett—"

"The others are here!" Michael yelled from the other side of the barge, interrupting them. "Joe, come join George and I and we'll give you a hand with your gear."

"Guess we'll continue this conversation in November," Joe Jelly said, and walked over to where Michael Ostend was holding up his bulky and heavy diving armor.

Lady Ostend smiled because she knew her husband

would, if he could, put on that gear and go into the water himself. She smiled, but the smile did not stop the shiver from going down her back when she considered what Mr. Jelly had almost just told her.

THANKS IN LARGE PART to Mr. Joseph Jelly's underwater salvage expertise, the Ostends and Mr. Hall were both very hopeful that money would be saved—earned in the case of Mr. Hall—by the amount of cargo reclaimed from the wreck. There was indeed a decent-sized pocket of air above the ripped hull and below the water's surface. Mr. Jelly was down there now, his armor on and his helmet off, directing the other divers who were tying ropes around the crates they could access and hooking each crate up to a line that ran through a pulley secured to a tripod tower on the *Argosy's* deck. Already there were twenty-seven crates piled on the barge's deck, most of them dry, a dozen stenciled with the words "Ostend & Sons Fine Silk Headwear/Clinton Falls, New York and Kingston, Ontario."

The winch had just been engaged to raise the twenty-eighth crate when Lady Ostend—along with everyone else on the boat, judging from their reactions—heard a creaking, then a snapping, then a splitting of wood. At first she thought it was the twenty-eighth crate, weakened by water, coming apart as it was being lifted out of the hold. Then George Hall and Michael ran to the front of the barge and looked down at the underside of the *Oconto's* bow. Just as suddenly, one of the divers popped his head up above water, unhitched his mask and flipped it open, and nervously announced that the hull was breaking apart.

"Get everyone out of there!" George Hall roared. "Get them out of there *now!*"

To assist the evacuation, George Hall, Michael Ostend and several others on the barge, including the insurance agent, fastened several strong ropes to the braces that ran under the barge's railing and tossed the other end of each rope into the water. Their quick thinking and swift action worked as one diver after another climbed on board while the timbers of the *Oconto* continued to crack and, now visibly to all, break.

"It's due to our shifting the weight of the cargo around," one of the divers said.

"Where's Mr. Jelly?" Michael Ostend asked.

"Dammit, he's still down there," George Hall replied.

"He didn't have his helmet on, either," the same diver added. "He was working in an open pocket, hitching the tackle up to the crates."

Michael Ostend had one shoe off and was already moving to the edge of the deck when George Hall stopped him with a strong hand on his shoulder. "Don't do it. We don't need to lose two of you today."

At the same time, Lady Ostend felt a wave of dizziness pass over her, then a clarity of vision that she had experienced only a couple of times before. She looked into the water. She felt the same sensation she remembered when she was talking to Mr. Jelly only an hour before, the sensation of seeing something, feeling something in the water.

"Tie the rope and air hose to the boom," Lady Ostend ordered.

Michael would later remark that she spoke with half the volume yet with twice the command as usual. George Hall hesitated for a second, as if he were going to protest against what was obviously a bad idea if Joe Jelly tried to put his helmet and breathing apparatus back on. One look from Lady Ostend stopped his words in his throat. He did as she ordered.

The *Oconto's* timbers continued to creak and crack and break. The men and one woman on the barge saw one deck board at a time split and pop in two. As each one broke the bow sank a little deeper.

Lady Ostend alone heard the wood of the stern and the metal of the propeller scour and scrape against the underwater shelf off of which it was falling. She also saw, in her mind's eye, Joe Jelly wrapping the rope and rubber air hose around his shoulders and arms. She could almost read his thoughts as he looked up and saw the glow of sunlight through the several compartments that had once been used to load and arrange cargo in the hold.

"If they do what I told them to do, and if the rope and rubber hold, we might just make it through this." To her surprise, Lady Ostend immediately realized that these were not Mr. Jelly's thoughts, but rather someone else's, someone who was in the water with the diver.

Suddenly, the decking started to snap more quickly, one board after another, several boards at once. At the same time, the heavier, tarred wood of the hull also started to snap, sending out sticky splinters in all directions, including onto the *Argosy's* deck. The water bubbled and churned. The bow straightened as it fell. The rope and rubber stretched and pulled against the force of sinking wood and churning water, but did not break.

"May God save you, Mr. Jelly," George Hall said.

Michael Ostend glanced over at the rope and air hose. "And may you hold on tight," he added.

Lady Ostend concentrated on seeing beyond the surface of the water, deep into the roiling river itself. It was almost as if she saw Joseph Jelly with something else's eyes.

"He's alive," she said to everyone's surprise, not least of all her husband's. "He has the rope and hose firmly tied around his shoulders. He's protecting his head with his arms. The boat is sinking around him. The compartment is filled up with water, but he's holding his breath. He's through one hole. He's lined up to move through another. He's through it. Now the final one, very difficult … he's hit his arm quite hard but he's reached a point of safety." Lady Ostend turned towards her husband. "Pull him the rest of the way," she said.

Michael Ostend, along with George Hall and two of the stronger divers, did just that.

When Joe Jelly reached the deck he rolled over onto his stomach, straightened his arms to get his head elevated and coughed until his lungs were cleared. He looked directly at Lady Ostend. "Glad you were listening," he said.

THE FIRST OSTEND BALL, held on Saturday, November 6, 1886, was as successful as anyone had dreamed it would be. It was a small affair compared to the extravagant soirees of later years, with only ten couples gathered around the table and with only four courses served on it. Yet it was as momentous an evening's gathering as any on the river before or since in any castle ballroom, if only for the stories that were traded and the seeds of connection that were sown.

Michael and Lady Ostend were there, of course, he in his elegant silk tuxedo and she in her taffeta and tulle. They hosted their first ball with the hospitable grace of two people completely at ease with each other and with what they shared between them. They welcomed each guest personally at the Valhalla boat house. They offered generous toasts and provided even more generously from their kitchen larder and wine cellar. They offered gifts to the staff, who had been preparing the feast for weeks. They thanked their guests for coming, reminding them that although the first week of November was not the easiest time to be on the river, it was the most rewarding time to be here, a fact of living that they hoped was reflected in their ball, the Ostend Ball.

Captain Doctor Charles Obadiah Smithson was there, guest of honor, Canadian hero, filled with tales of the Western Canadian wilderness, of Crimea, and of Civil War America. Most special, of course, were his tales of Egypt and the Sudan, where he had met and had befriended the mysterious and seemingly ageless Naguib Malqari, who had told Captain Doctor Smithson about the strange golden powder that Napoleon Bonaparte himself had sent to the New World and was now in, and a life-enhancing part of, the Saint Lawrence River.

The painter Frederick Remington was there, too. He delighted in the Ostends' hospitality. He listened carefully to Captain Doctor Smithson's story, that first year and every year thereafter. He listened and learned, and when he returned to his lonely cabin in Chippewa Bay he listened and watched. He never said whether he heard or saw or felt any of the water-beings whose lives were so closely entwined to Napoleon's gold. But he did express their meaning in paint —the glorious portrait of Lady Ostend among the elements that he completed in 1892, just in time for the seventh annual Ostend Ball.

And Joseph Jelly was there, as he would be for every Ostend Ball that followed until his death in old age. And every year he told the story of his dramatic escape from the *Oconto*. Did he embellish the drama? Sure he did—he was, after all, a recreational fisherman as well as a professional diver. In later retellings he was in the stern of the *Oconto*, taking inventory of the bloom iron that had slid down from its original location when the boat went bow up. He was trapped in the iron when the ship began to sink the second time, he said, struggling to keep his head, then face, then mouth and nose, then nose alone in the diminishing air pocket above him. He sprung himself forward by using his rubber breathing hose like a slingshot, he said, and he was lucky that his aim was perfect because he barely slipped through six doorways before popping his head out of the water and asking his late great employer, George Hall, for a double shot of rum.

Lady Ostend listened to Joe Jelly's story year after year, nodding with approval and smiling as she recognized a new detail, an embellished moment, a reconfigured truth. At the same time, she knew that by reworking the story Mr. Jelly was only trying to comprehend what was truly incomprehensible, because she, and she alone, saw what had really happened that day in July 1886.

When Joe Jelly told his story for the first time that year, hesitatingly, obviously confused and perhaps not wanting to know what really happened, Lady Ostend saw the nods given by Captain Smithson, Mr. Remington, Mrs. Bourne and several other guests at her table. She knew that they knew what she was only beginning to learn—that the Saint Lawrence River concealed many secrets that a lifetime of disciplined study might, just might, reveal.

Borderland: A Brief History

of the Thousand Islands

(April 1989)

Melinda McDonnell
Expository Writing Essay
Advanced Placement English Composition
Mr. Farber
April 4, 1989

BACK WHEN I WAS A LITTLE GIRL, the tour guides used to say that if you paid attention and looked closely enough you could see the international border painted on the river floor. Once—I think I was nine—the captain of the cruise boat we were on let me steer right along what he said was the boundary. "A little to the left," He'd say. "No back to the right. Oops, a smidgen too far. There you go. Steady, steady. Now you're there!" He tussled my hair. "Believe it or not, little miss Mindy, you've now got one foot in America and one foot in Canada!" I think I believed him.

Now I know better. I go on the tour boats now and I hear the guides say the international border is white or yellow or orange. Inevitably, at least a quarter of the passengers peer over the gunwale, some actually with binoculars, some with their video cameras, to try and see it. Most of them get the joke pretty quickly. The thick ones keep looking, as if the Powers-That-Be on either side could really paint a borderline on the river floor. Who knows? Maybe they think they can. Maybe some of us, wanting more from our leaders than they can provide, wish they could.

Another tour boat tall-tale is that the ten-foot bridge between Big Zavikon and Little Zavikon Islands is actually the smallest international bridge in the world. I used to believe this one too when I was little. I remember asking the captain where the border patrol booth was. He said that this one was so important for international security that they only patrolled it by air. He told me that whenever someone needed to cross, like if a little girl named Mindy on Little Zavikon needed to go back to Big Zavikon for lunch, a helicopter would hover just above the bridge, and a Royal Canadian Mounted Policeman would rappel down a rope and ask little Mindy all kinds of questions about where she was going, how long she was staying there, what she was bringing into Canada, who her parents were, if she brushed her teeth twice a day and ate her vegetables, etc., etc., etc. Maybe it was on the same tour that I got to straddle the international border, maybe not. I do remember asking the captain if the horse came down from the helicopter with the Royal Canadian Mounted Policeman. He looked at me as if I were nuts. He said, "little miss Mindy, everyone knows that horses prefer airplanes."

The border jokes are good jokes precisely because they're so absurd. When it comes to people in their boats, or muskellunges under the water, or algae on the surface, or the water itself for that matter, there is no border. The map says there is, of course, and the guards between the bridges and on their boats try to enforce what the map says. But for practical purposes the Thousand Islands exist in a strange and amorphous rift between two nations, not quite totally belonging to either, yet constantly flowing into and ebbing back from the other. It's a pretty fluid borderland.

For practical purposes, the fluidity of the border

between New York in America and Ontario in Canada has proved both advantageous and problematic; advantageous for criminals who use the hidden intricacies of the border for their crimes, problematic for the authorities on both sides who try to stop them.

Today, the most significant border-related illegal activity is smuggling cigarettes and human trafficking. According to the statistics, both activities are more prevalent in the northeastern New York-southwestern Ontario section of the border, especially on the St. Regis Indian reservation. Times are tough there, and a bitter resentment remains towards both American and Canadian authorities for round after round of ill-treatment in the past. More than anything, I find it sad that the St. Regis people feel forced to resort to such desperate crimes. But I cannot judge, nor can I condemn them for feeling that they have so few other options.

In a different category altogether is the most significant illegal activity of past times on the upper part of the river[*]— Prohibition-era liquor smuggling. These border-crossing malefactors were hardly ever desperate, just thirsty. They brought rum, gin and whiskey from Canada under the cover of night or fog. They eluded federal agents more often than not by slipping between islands or into a secret cove. Not even the oldest River Rat knows how many small inlets along the shores of islands or the mainland have earned the name "Smuggler's Cove." If the smugglers were very clever, they would outfit their boats with secret compartments that the authorities could not find. If worse came to worse they would simply dump their stash overboard, and perhaps try to retrieve it the next day. Legend has it that there are still

---

[*]The Saint Lawrence River flows in a northeasterly direction from Lake Ontario to the Gulf of Saint Lawrence. Thus, the Upper Saint Lawrence, the Thousand Islands section, is to the southwest of the Lower Saint Lawrence, which starts at Montreal and goes to the Gulf of Saint Lawrence. It may be counter-intuitive with our habit of placing north at the top of our maps, but that's the way it is.

cases of whiskey on the river floor, waiting for the enter-
prising (or desperate) drinker to find them.

Even further back in time was a pirate, William Johnston, who made a name for himself that, later, many a
Prohibition-era smuggler would envy. Johnston was an all-
around pest to law enforcement authorities on both sides of
the border. In America he recruited soldiers to join his "Pat-
riot's Army" that would attack Canada and assert the
independence of the river people themselves. On the shore
of Wellesley Island he blew up the *Sir Robert Peel*, allegedly
by mistake as he and his men were robbing it of the pay-
master's gold it carried. He ended up hiding from the
authorities in an island cave. Eventually, the authorities con-
cluded that they could keep a better eye on him if they gave
him a job as lighthouse keeper, a post he held until the day
he died. Johnston faithfully carried the torch of previous
skirmishes in the region. The War of 1812, the American
Revolution and the French and Indian War all had battles of
one degree or another on this border between two nations.

It was a geological border that made the river and its islands such a boon for smugglers, scoundrels and soldiers
and such a perpetual source of anxiety for law enforcement
officials. The oldest rocks in the area are about a billion
years old, give or take fifty million years. They are sedimentary rocks like sandstone and shale that were buried under
layer upon layer of more rock until pressure and heat meta-
morphosized them into marbles, quartzites, gneisses and
schists. Millions of years after that, igneous rocks like granite pushed up into the morphed sedimentary rock. This
pushing-up pushed everything up—six hundred million
years ago a tall, Himalaya-like mountain chain existed
roughly along the same southwest to northeast axis that the
river runs today.

Wind and water eroded those mountains. What we
know as the Thousand Islands archipelago is what remains
of those mountains' bases. The colorful rock we see in

several road cuts along Interstate 81 on Wellesley Island or in the cliff edges of hundreds of islands up and down the river are exposed remnants of the hard granites and gneisses that water and wind could not completely erode. They are tinted pink because of their high iron content, the iron being oxidized by its contact with the air. These Precambrian igneous outcrops are also part of the Frontenac Arch or Axis, a relatively narrow swath of rock that connects the much larger Algonquin Dome in Canada with the Adirondack Dome in New York. It was the hardness of the Frontenac Arch that resisted the eroding action of glaciers and water and allowed this section of the Saint Lawrence River to have so many more islands than other sections of the river that ran through softer rock. Hard rock/soft rock —another border, this time literally in the land.

Erosion leveled the old Precambrian mountains. Wind and water deposited sand, which solidified into layer upon layer of sedimentary rock. Two large basins, which became lakes when filled with water, developed on either side of the old, hard rock of the Frontenac Arch. The relatively flat and undramatic landscape of Wolfe and Howe Islands is a geological testament to this long process of deposition and erosion.

The same process also set the stage for the Pleistocene glaciers, which covered the entire area with ice several miles deep until the ice started to melt around fifteen to seventeen thousand years ago. The Frontenac Arch border dictated the transition from glacial ice sheet to glacial lake—Lake Iroquois and the Champlain Sea formed on either side of it. Lake Iroquois would shrink and be renamed Lake Ontario. The Champlain Sea would shrink and break up into the lower Saint Lawrence River, the Gulf of Saint Lawrence and Lake Champlain. For a time, probably around twelve thousand years ago, there was an even more complex borderland in the region with water to the southwest and northeast (Lake Iroquois and the Champlain Sea), glacier-free dry land to the south, and the still massive, still very cold Laurentian Ice Sheet to the north. Once all the ice melted, once all the glacial lakes shrunk into just lakes, the water that remained and the rocks that protruded from it formed what we know today as the Thousand Islands. The glaciers left their mark —what the French called, poetically, *roche moutonnee*, and what we call, blandly, "sheep backs" are telltale signs of glacial erosion. Many of our 1,864-ish islands slope gradually on one side, "up-ice," and sharply and irregularly on another side, "down-ice." Thank the glaciers next time you enjoy cliff-jumping on a hot August afternoon.

There's a final border in the Thousand Islands region that's substantially harder to pin down, at least using the techniques of history or geology. Perhaps the best way to explain it is to tell a story.

We were on vacation (obviously) at Wellesley Island State Park. I was playing with my doll, named Shelly, at the water's edge. She was the kind of doll that closed her eyes when you tipped her backwards. I had her practicing her backstroke in the water—I remember that because her eyes were closed. Shelly and I were the only ones there. All the other kids had gone back to their campsites for dinner. My mom and I were about to go back to ours too because my dad was grilling hot dogs and my sister and brother had gone with him to help. I remember that because my mom had just given me my ten minute warning. We were also leaving the next day, so I *really* didn't want to get out of the water. I said this to Shelly.

"I don't want you to go, either," is the reply I heard.

I stood Shelly up. Her eyes opened. Let me make one thing clear: Shelly was *not* the kind of doll with the string in the back who talked when you pulled it. I was playing in the water. My mom had warned me that playing in the water with Chrissy, the doll that talked, would ruin her, so I left Chrissy at home to watch over things.

I looked back at my mom. She waved. "Ten minutes,

honey," she said. She obviously didn't want to go either and had decided to stop time. She was still in the same spot, still halfway up the hill, still reading her *Good Housekeeping* and gazing out at the river, probably thinking how little she wanted to get back to doing real housekeeping. She wasn't the one who said "I don't want you to go, either," either. I knew that much.

I held Shelly tight and walked further into the water a couple steps. Danny Channing, our across-the-street neighbor back home who also came up to the Thousand Islands, usually two weeks before we did, was fond of telling me about the eels that he saw in the water, here at Wellesley Island Park, in Alex Bay, in Clayton, on boat tours, while water skiing—listen to Danny Channing and you'd think the river was filled with eels and only eels. I hated eels. So for me to walk up to my thighs in that allegedly eel-infested water without either of my parents was a pretty big deal. But there were no eels. Nor fish. Only a voice that said again, "I don't want you to go, either." Small waves were coming in from the wakes of the boats that passed far away. To my eyes there were other waves happening too as the river spoke, waves going both with and against the natural ebb and flow.

The story has no real ending. My dad came back down to the swimming area and told us that the hot dogs were ready. My mom said, "Dinner time sweetie. Come on out of the water and dry yourself off." I obeyed. Both my parents knew something was up because I didn't want any s'mores. My sister and brother knew something was up because I didn't return their teasing. Thankfully, all of them assumed I was down in the dumps because we were going home the following day. I was, of course. But I was also kind of shell-shocked. Numbed. There was no way I would have articulated it like this back then, but I knew I had just had a spiritual experience. I knew that the border between here and there had just been breached right before my eyes. It never happened again. Once was probably enough.

The border between here and there is the "substantially harder to pin down" borderland I mentioned earlier. I don't want to call it a supernatural border because that just gets too complicated. It's a liminal border, I guess, just below, or beyond, our conscious awareness. It's a border between here and there, between earth and heaven, between the seen and the unseen, between this world and an "otherworld," between what we can reach out and touch with our hands and what we can feel only with our hearts. Geology can't explain it, although we should keep in mind that in the Thousand Islands ancient rock shaped by fire is kissed, day after day, moment after moment, by the other two elements of air and water. Perhaps it's a spiritual Frontenac Arch, connecting what we know and do now with what's happening on another plane of existence.

History can't explain this liminal border, either, but it can help confirm that it's there. The original inhabitants of the Thousand Islands knew about this particular borderland. In fact, to them it was the only one that mattered since neither America nor Canada existed back then, and when the countries did exist the Native Americans didn't recognize their sovereignty anyway. They called the Thousand Islands "God's Garden." They said that the islands themselves were tears that fell from God's eyes at the rending of the world. They carved petroglyphs on the ancient cliff walls as a testament to what they learned from things they did not see.

There's a reason why tourist attractions spring up where they do. It's not only natural beauty or geography or ease of access. The reason why the Thousand Islands region was so popular in the Gilded Age and is again since the 1960's is that people want to be here. Why else would the Pullmans, Emerys, Bournes, Ostends, Strausses, Boldts and so many other rich and famous families choose to build their mansions and castles here? They, and modern day sunbathers and water-skiers as well, might not recognize it consciously (hence liminal) but they do become drawn to a place because it offers them what ordinary, everyday life cannot.

A Hindu swami understood it when he came to the Thousand Islands in the late 1800's and opened a retreat house that remains active today. Christians from all over the world understand it when, on Sunday afternoons, they worship in the water at Half Moon Bay, beside the Precambrian pink granite cliffs and beneath the open sky of the "world's tallest cathedral." Children, especially, understand it because they are still in tune with the unseen things around them.

I certainly experienced it on that summer day of my seventh year on this earth, as I stood on the edge of an ancient rock and looked down into the water shared by two great nations. I stood at three different borderlands at once that day—the historical, the geological and the spiritual. On that day, I experienced everything that the Thousand Islands had to offer.

Melinda,

You demonstrate great clarity of thought and organization through most of this essay. Your transition from idea to outline to essay has been a very smooth process. What happened to your original ending? Explaining the origins of Thousand Islands dressing would have been a much stronger conclusion, more rooted in the reality of the here and now, and more indicative of the place you so expertly describe in the first two sections of your essay. A culinary border, if you will, between haute cuisine *and the ordinary food of the masses. As it is, your exposition loses much of its force when you move away from hard and clear facts. Remember this advice in September —keep your feet firmly planted on the ground. Stick with history or geology, or both if you can handle a double major. In the end, you'll be happy that you did!* **B-**

Andrew Hibbard Rides the Wake

(August 2002)

ON A HOT, HAZY DAY IN AUGUST 2002, Andrew Hibbard pulled his Crestliner up to the dock at Heron's Nest and secured the boat to the moorings. He jumped onto the dock, where his someday-to-be cousin-in-law was sunbathing, reading and enjoying an afternoon cocktail in a chaise lounge. "Hey ho, Min. What's up?"

Mindy McDonnell put the book down. "*You* took a day off?" she said.

"Nope. Started early. Got a full day in."

"Full day? What time is it?" Mindy looked to the southwest and, even with sunglasses on, shielded her eyes.

"Three o'clock in the PM."

"Thought so. You started work when?"

"On the job at 4:30. Building a seawall for some rich Canadian who doesn't want her petunias splashed by the tour boats. Don't need much light to stack rocks."

Mindy laughed. "Tom's inside. Beer is too."

"Not today," Andrew replied with a shake of his head.

"Mark the calendar!" Mindy exclaimed. "What's the occasion? Or should I say anti-occasion?"

"I've got some serious boating to do," Andrew said. He went inside and found his cousin in the basement, washing out the brushes he'd been using to paint the screened porch's trim. "Hey, cuz. Knockin' off for the day?"

"Hot one. Time for a swim." Tom Flanagan took note

of Andrew's fluorescent orange swimsuit and flower-patterned purple shirt. "You look ready."

"I've got something better than swimming for you."

"What, you put up a water slide?"

"Even better than that." Andrew smiled. "The *Bellerophon's* headed downriver, full of grain. Rick Reynolds is piloting. ETA in your front yard: fifteen minutes."

Tom Flanagan turned off the water and started drying the brushes with an old cotton washcloth. "Okay. And?"

"You remember the *Bellerophon*, right? From last September? When you came to visit me in your kayak?"

"How could I forget? Your little game with the bell nearly gave me a heart attack."

"The ship's full. It's got new dual props. Ricky Rey rarely obeys the speed limits."

Tom sighed. "I'm guessing you didn't drive your truck over."

"Come on, man, it's August. This is the opportunity of the summer. The thrill of a lifetime."

Tom hung the brushes on nails in the wall above the sink. "I can't, Andrew. We're supposed to meet the Slatterys for dinner. I've got to get cleaned up and ..."

"What time?"

"7:00. At Foxy's."

"I'll have you back here by 5:30. We'll go down to the bridge and back." He held up two fingers. "Two hours tops."

"Swear?"

"Swear."

"All right. Let me change into some shorts."

Andrew pointed at the brushes. "You don't have to wash them every night, you know. Put a little paint on them, stick them in an old bread bag, tie the bag around the handle and put it in the fridge. Next day you start right where you left off. It's like you never stopped. Get changed. I'll be in the boat."

Andrew was stowing some gear when Tom, wearing olive green swim trunks and a grey New York Yankees shirt, arrived at the dock. "Where you off to?" Mindy asked as Tom untethered the moorings.

"Ridin' the wake," Andrew said. "Wanna come?"

"No thanks." Mindy rolled her eyes. "Just have him back …"

"I know," Andrew interrupted. He lowered his wrap-around sunglasses and looked over them. "Dinner at seven. He'll be back by 5:30."

"I was going to say have him back in one piece."

Andrew reversed the boat away from the shore, turned around, and throttled up. He stopped when they reached the deeper part of the channel. "You're lucky," he said.

"Why?" Tom asked.

"Great section of the river you've got here. Historic. *Vickery* is over there." He pointed as he spoke. "*Oconto* over there. *Iroquoise*, the old one, over there. Ever seen 'em?"

"The only one I've seen is the *Islander.*"

"Kid's stuff."

"I've never been into diving."

He pointed back towards shore. "You remember what's over there, right?"

"The cave where our grandparents saw the gold," Tom Flanagan said. "Another place I've never visited."

"Me either," Andrew said. "Billy was supposed to take me this summer. Guess I'm on my own now. You two ever getting hitched?"

"Mindy and I?"

"No, you and Billy Masterson's effin' ghost. Of course you and Mindy."

Tom was laughing. "We are. We just don't know when yet. We're putting our lives in order first. I'm getting my business up and running. Mindy's making the transition from Buffalo back to Clinton Falls. We're renovating the cottage."

Andrew pointed back towards shore. "Mindy's sunbathing on your dock with chick-lit in one hand and a frozen margarita in another. Looks to me like she's got her life pretty much in order." Andrew stared at his cousin, his eyes hidden by the dark glasses. "You really think you'll find your brother?" he finally asked. "You really think he'll see one of your ads and call you up?"

"We had to do something."

"We? This is you, cuz. Mindy might be going along for the ride because she loves you, but you can't expect that to last."

"Hopefully it'll last forever."

"I'm not talking about the love. I'm talking about going along for the ride."

"She says she'll help me for as long as it takes."

"She says. She's fickle, though, like all women. Maybe not as fickle as the rest, but still. Sooner or later what she says now won't hold water."

"We'll see." Tom glanced upriver, hoping to end the conversation. He saw a ship approaching in the distance. "Is that the *Bellerophon*?"

Andrew raised his sunglasses to take a look. "Yup. Let's go meet her. She ain't fickle." He put the boat in gear and hit the throttle. "Let me know if things get rough. She listens to me. I'll have your back."

"You always have," Tom said.

"I want the best for you guys, you know. She's good for you, and vice versa."

"I appreciate that," Tom said. "But can we have some fun now?"

Andrew flashed a wide grin. "You bet your ass we can." Still facing his cousin, he reached to his side and throttled up so quickly that Tom was thrown onto his backside, and almost into the water. "Get your sea legs on, sailor!" Andrew yelled.

Tom grabbed hold of the transom and came to a knee. "Warn me next time," he said, laughing nevertheless.

"I did," Andrew said.

Tom moved up to the bow and took a seat on the port side, next to Andrew and the steering wheel. He felt good being out on the river, something he and Mindy seldom did in high summer because of the boat traffic and general noise. But boats were sparse on this day, perhaps because of the scorching late afternoon heat. The heat and breeze and spray of the river water all felt good, though. Tom was glad he was here.

Andrew slowed the boat as they approached the freighter, but only so Tom could hear him over the noise of the small boat's motor and the ship's engine. "The thing I like about the *Bellerophon* is that its wake is wackier than most. Pay attention as we get closer. I'll take you across its prow and then we'll catch the bow-wake going backwards for a while."

"So the waves will be coming from behind us?"

"Bingo. Don't worry if water comes over the transom. It'll take more than a few gallons to sink this tub."

Andrew did exactly as he said, taking them within twenty feet of the huge freighter's steel prow, with the ship coming at them the whole time. While Tom gazed up at the immensity of the pointed steel wall above him and to his right, he wondered if the captain, Rick Reynolds—"Ricky Rey" Andrew called him—knew what was happening in front of the vessel he was charged to safely pilot downriver.

"Hang on!" Andrew yelled. Then he turned sharply to the starboard, bringing the hull of his boat right up into the large, fast wake of the freighter. Tom hung on, planting his feet firmly on the deck and gripping the back of the seat with both his left and right hands. He still felt like he was going to fly out of the boat. The splash of water that drenched him from his left side only added to the feeling of impending inundation. He closed his eyes.

The Crestliner righted itself as it reached the crest of the wake. Then the bottom dropped out, and Tom felt his center of gravity falling backwards. He swore he felt the surface of the river's water brush the side of his head. Tom opened his eyes as the boat settled on the outside edge of the wave. He saw Andrew looking up towards the pilot house of the *Bellerophon*, pumping both his arms like a bad dancer on karaoke night. Tom knew what was coming and covered his ears with his hands. The alternating long blast, short blast, long blast, short blast was still incredibly loud.

"Does that mean something?" Tom yelled.

"Ricky Rey sees us and gives us the all-clear. Now we can have some real fun."

Just as Andrew spoke the words the *Bellerophon* accelerated noticeably. Andrew throttled up too, and steered his boat upriver along the starboard hull of the freighter with the *Bellerophon's* bow wake well to the Crestliner's port. Tom saw his cousin brace himself and at the same time saw the freighter's trailing wake directly ahead. He tightened his grip, too.

Andrew's Crestliner hit the trailing wake with a thwack and was propelled upwards over the crest. Tom let out the first exclamation, then Andrew responded with a "Yeah!" of his own. Back and forth Andrew steered them over the trailing wake. Up and down they went like a couple of kids enjoying a new carnival ride with no parent there to slow them down or scold them for their recklessness.

Andrew slowed his boat when they reached a point far behind the freighter. He turned around so they faced downriver. "Whadd'ya think?" he asked Tom with a wide grin on his face.

"More fun than I thought," Tom said.

"Flat bottom boats, they make the rockin' world go round," Andrew sang with a burst of air guitar. "I'll take one just like this over a deep-hulled speedboat any day."

"Are we done?"

"Hardly."

"Good. Can we do some more of those jumps?"

Andrew's expression flattened to one of insincere seriousness. "We're adults, cuz. We're done with that kid's stuff. Now I'm going to show you something *really* interesting."

Feeling good, Tom wondered what that something really interesting would be.

It didn't take long for them to catch up to the freighter, which had slowed down as it approached the Rock Island Lighthouse. Andrew slowed, too, and concentrated as he positioned his boat to where he wanted it in relation to the larger vessel in front of him.

"What are you doing?" Tom asked. "We're going awfully slow."

"What we just did was jump the wake. Like I said, that's kid's stuff. Now we're going to ride the wake." Andrew pointed towards shore. "Your honey's watching. Give her a wave."

Mindy was watching, even though she usually feigned disinterest in seaway traffic. Tom gave her a salute and she responded with a queen's wave. He blew her a kiss and she caught it.

Meanwhile, Andrew steered the keel slowly back and forth, aligning the bow of his boat to the trailing wake of the *Bellerophon*. He let off the throttle and slowed down even more. "Almost got it," he said quietly, "almost there. Got it. Now, Thomas, look over the gunwhale."

Tom started to move to his left then hesitated. "You gonna swerve into the wave and knock me overboard?"

"With Mindy watching? You kidding me? I'd never hear the end of it. We're riding the wake, cuz. The objective now is to see how long I can hold it. Slow and steady now."

Tom stood up, grabbed hold of the gunwale trim and leaned his head out over the water. He looked into the water for about two minutes, then turned around to face Andrew. "We're floating," he said.

"Pretty much. My guess is there's about six inches of boat on the wave's crest. That's all that's holding us up. As long as I keep us centered on that six inches, the rest of us is floating, like you said. Just stay where you are on that side of the boat. And try not to rock too much."

Tom was astonished at how peaceful the feeling was, despite the *Bellerophon's* engine noise and occasional whiff of exhaust fumes. He'd always loved the rocking motion of being out in his kayak in a light swell. This was like that but even more gentle. It felt to him as if the river were taking care of them.

"Some people do this while windsurfing," Andrew said. "Can you imagine?"

"No, I can't. Ever try it on a jet ski?"

"Once." Andrew shook his head. "I've always found jet skis more annoying than fun, though. As I said, I prefer my flat-bottoms over everything else, at least for this activity."

"Now I know why," Tom said. He returned to the gunwale and watched the water. It corkscrewed as it moved below them, churning downward and outward as it approached the shore. "How fast are we going?" he asked.

"Fifteen," Andrew replied. "Like I said, Ricky Rey likes to speed. He's taking it easy today, though. The Coast Guard might be out. I've seen him blow through here at twenty-five to thirty. Pisses the cottage owners off."

"And you?" Tom asked, noticing that we were approaching Hibbard Island. "Does it piss you off?"

"I'm on an island. I had a choice. I built my dock on the non-channel side."

"You said the Coast Guard's out?"

"Maybe."

"Will we get in trouble for this?"

"Not at this distance. Besides, they know me. They know I'm not one of those drunken idiot jet skiers."

"How much farther we going?"

Andrew looked at his watch. "Just a little bit more. Let me do one more thing. Hold on. I'll try to keep this gentle. I'll try."

Andrew gave the steering wheel just a flick to the right. The boat dropped from crest to trough, with Tom's stomach along with it. The drop was even more dramatic than the one they took when they were jumping the wake, although it didn't put them off balance. They were directly behind the freighter's keel now.

"Feel that? Feel us being pulled down?" Andrew asked.

"That's weird," Tom said.

"And this is exactly where you don't want to be on a jet ski," Andrew said. "Get much closer than we are on one of them and you will be pulled down. Then you'll have the prop to deal with."

"It's deceptively calm for such a dangerous place," Tom said. And looking overboard it seemed to him that the water wasn't moving at all between the two wakes. "To be in motion yet at the same time so still."

"Ridin' the wake," Andrew said. "Not bad, huh?"

They were almost right under the bridge now. When Andrew put the boat in neutral, Tom felt the sensation of coming to a stop. Gradually, the boat began to sway as the *Bellerophon* continued downriver, taking it's wake with it.

"Later," Andrew said, saluting the ship.

They sat silent for a few minutes, the thwoop of the freighter's engines quieting in the distance.

"Here we are," Andrew eventually said.

Tom was fairly certain he knew what his cousin was talking about. He looked up and watched a pickup and camper cross to the mainland. "Do you miss him?" he asked when the truck and trailer were finally out of view.

Andrew nodded. "Every day. I'd see him at least three or four times a week, you know, somewhere on the river. Some days he'd stop by a job and mooch some lunch. Or some days we'd fish or just go out for a ride. In the fall we'd dive a little."

"You ever ride the wake together?"

"Who do you think taught me? Back when you had your nose stuck in some Clinton Falls archive, I was out here with Billy learning all the tricks." Andrew laughed softly. "And drinking." He laughed again. "We were idiots then."

Tom was looking down into the water. Above them, on the bridge, the eighteen wheelers clip-clopped their rhythm over the steel joints between pavement slabs.

"I have a hard time going to Jimmy's these days," Andrew said.

Tom nodded. "We know. We miss you." A large fiberglass yacht, bound upriver and flying the Canadian flag, passed them and set them rolling in its wake. "We also understand."

As the wake from the yacht dissipated Andrew slid his glasses up above his forehead and looked from shore to shore. "Can I tell you something in confidence?" he asked.

"Of course."

He lowered his glasses and turned the ignition off. He and Tom floated in the gentle swell. "I've been seeing things," he said slowly.

"What sort of things?" Tom asked.

"It's hard to explain."

"Just tell me about it."

"I was riding the wake a few weeks ago, like we were doing just now. I was going in the other direction, though, following the *Argoma* upriver. Going nice and slow, nice and steady, keeping my balance, and I ..." Andrew paused. Tom waited. "I don't know. I just don't know how to describe it."

"Was it an undine?"

"In August? In the American Narrows? Not a chance!" Andrew pointed down towards the water, then looked up to the sky. "Besides, he ... it wasn't in the water, at least at first. It started out like a storm cloud. Very dark and moving east. Billowing, too. What I saw then made me get off the wake and stop my boat."

"Good idea in a storm."

"No. Turns out it wasn't a storm. It started to take shape. First legs, then a torso, then arms and a head ..."

"The storm cloud turned into a person?"

"No. Well, yes. I saw him ... it ... descend to the bridge and grow bigger."

"How big?"

"Really big eventually. He straddled the bridge, Tom. He had both legs in the water." Andrew swallowed. "You know how impossible that is? You know how deep it is here?"

Tom looked down, felt dizzy and returned his gaze to his cousin. "Hundred-fifty feet?"

Andrew nodded.

"What did you do?"

"I freaked out. Almost fell into the water." Andrew shook his head. "I don't know. I was scared. I thought I was hallucinating. You know, tweaking. But he was real, like some dreams are more real than being awake. You know what I mean? He looked so *real*, man. I restarted the motor and high-tailed it back upriver."

"Did you look back at the bridge? See him do anything?"

"Hell no!"

"Were you drinking?"

"Not before it happened. I had plenty to drink after."

"That's understandable. You went back home?"

"My plan was to go over to Foxy's. But I didn't get there because I saw something else as I caught up to the *Argoma*."

"What else?" Tom asked.

"I saw it out of the corner of my eye. A glint. Or a flash. Like when the sun reflects off somebody's wristwatch and moves across the wall. I saw it just for a second. I turned my head to get a closer look. It was Billy."

"*What?* Seriously?"

"Believe it or not, he was riding the wake, right next to me. He was lying down, though, like he was on a surfboard. He was invisible, too, but not quite." Andrew snapped his fingers. "Cellophane. That's it. I saw him, but I also saw through him like he was made of Saran Wrap."

"Did he look at you?"

"Maybe."

"Did he look like Billy?"

"Hard to say with the water there. He was skinny, I know that much."

"Did he wave? Splash water your way? Anything?"

"No. It was like he couldn't move the way we do. Like he didn't have arms to wave or legs to paddle with or a head to turn my way and speak. I don't know. It was hard to tell with the distance and the waves and with me trying to keep my balance. But ..."

"But what?"

Andrew hesitated.

"He said something, didn't he?"

"No. Not like you and I talk. I *felt* him tell me something, though. I couldn't hear it with my ears, but I heard it inside me."

"Voices in your head?"

"No. Not like that at all."

"Like what then?"

"You know how somebody tells you something and it makes you feel a certain way emotionally? It was like that. I felt him say it."

"What did he say?"

"He said a change is comin'. He said it's gonna be big, like the guy over the bridge."

"Did you look? Was the big guy still there?"

Andrew shook his head. "No way. Besides, Billy was

still talking. He told me to pay attention because it was important. He told me to keep ridin' the wake. He said I'll be okay if I keep ridin' the wake. Just like that, just like the old Billy would've said it."

"Keep ridin' the wake."

"Yeah. Keep ridin' the wake." Andrew paused. "Know what I did?"

"What?"

"I kept ridin' the wake."

"That day?"

Andrew nodded. "That's why I never made it to Foxy's."

"How far'd you ride it?" Tom asked.

"All the way to Cape Vincent."

"*What?*" Tom rocked the boat as he stood up.

"I tailed the *Argoma* all the way to Cape Vincent," Andrew explained.

"That's what, twenty miles?"

"Give or take."

"You're insane!"

"Billy told me to keep ridin' the wake. I was so freaked out by the big guy over the bridge that I did what he said, especially since it meant continuing in the other direction. I kept it up as far as I could, all the way to Cape Vincent. I was running out of gas, though. It was getting choppy up there, too. There's no way I was taking this little boat out into Lake Ontario with an empty gas tank."

Tom shook his head and laughed.

"What's so funny?"

"You. You rode the wake all the way to Cape Vincent? Because Billy's ghost told you to do it? And then you *stopped?*"

"You're one to talk with your Cornflower's ghost ..."

"No, that's not what I mean. What I'm saying is that you probably should have trusted him. If he wanted you to keep riding the wake you should have kept riding the wake.

Don't get me wrong, you probably set a new Thousand Islands record for distance, but there might have been so much more."

"Like what? Another cloud giant riding the Wolfe Island ferry?"

Tom laughed. "I don't know, maybe he was leading you to something. Seems to me that Billy Masterson, alive or dead, would not tell you to do something that would bring you harm. Close to it, maybe, close enough to make it fun, but not close enough to actually hurt you."

"Good point. So maybe I should catch the next ship going back upriver. Wait for it up near Clayton and make sure my tank is full."

"Not until after you take me home," Tom said. "What time is it, anyway?"

"Quarter to five," Andrew said. "I'll take you home. And I'll wait for another day to ride the wake out to Ontario." He turned the key and fired up the ignition. "You don't think I'm nuts?"

"Not because you saw a ghost," Tom answered with a smile. "There's plenty of other reasons, but that's not one of them."

Andrew laughed. "I don't seek advice much, but I'm glad I came to you. Thanks for hearing me out. It feels good to get that off my chest."

"You're welcome," Tom said. "You want some advice?"

"What?"

"Keep ridin' the wake."

Andrew laughed. "Wanna drive?" he asked.

"Love to," Tom said with a smile.

The cousins made their way back upriver, silently enjoying the combination of warm sun and cool breeze on their faces. Tom Flanagan was thinking about his missing brother, as he so often did these days. Tomorrow he and Mindy would meet with a captain from the New York State Police.

He had a good feeling that the meeting would provide him with some clues to Patrick's whereabouts.

Andrew Hibbard had half his mind back on business, thinking about how much of that seawall he could build to-morrow and how many days it would take him to finish the job. While his mind was on his job he was also feeling the river, enjoying it—really enjoying it—for the first time since the upheavals of the previous fall.

Keep ridin' the wake, Billy had said. Andrew would do just that, metaphorically if not literally. After he dropped his cousin off at Heron's Nest, the river cottage that their great-grandfather had built with his own hands, he'd go back to Hibbard Island, pack himself a dinner and some beers, and return to Tom's section of the river to cast for some small-mouth bass in the shallow water off Rock Island Shoal. If he saw another giant he'd wish it well and offer him a Moosehead. If a freighter came by upriver he might, just might, ride its wake as far as the water and wind would take him.

A Birth on the River

(December 24/25, 1962)

THE KNOCK ON THE DOOR COMES FIRST, and startles me, perhaps more than it should. I am back at home after a lovely Christmas Eve service. I find the Methodist Christmas Eve service the most lovely of them all because Methodist preachers usually know when to keep their sermons short. Christmas Eve is a time for congregational singing, not for preaching, and singing "lustily and with a good courage" is the second reason why I find the Methodist Christmas Eve service the most lovely of them all. Yes, we have a choir. Yes, they like to present their anthem—*anthems* on Christmas Eve—with all the sentimental drama they can muster. But tonight's service is about the hymns, sometimes, including this year, practically all of them that can be found in the most recent version of the Hymnal. We sing about peace, even though peace is as far away as it has ever been. We sing about angels, even though for many in the congregation angels exist only in the imagination. We sing about the Christ child's birth as if it were happening tonight rather than tomorrow. But as my late husband used to say, "it's tomorrow somewhere, dearie." I suppose it's yesterday somewhere, too. I also suppose that if you add up all those yesterdays, todays and tomorrows, you might understand something about why the Christ child's birth still matters.

I am sitting in my chair beside a fire, singing "'Twas in

the Moon of Wintertime," lustily and with a good bit of courage, when the knock comes at the door. I am annoyed at the interruption because the hymn is one of my favourites and because its rhythm helps me maintain the rhythm of my tatting. I have yards upon yards of it to finish for the border of a quilt we're supposed to have ready for the Epiphany bazaar. The knock continues, louder and quicker. The knock causes me to stop singing just as the chiefs arrived with their gifts. I lose track of the hymn and thus lose track of my pattern.

Next comes the chiming of the clock. It's an elaborate Edwardian piece handed down through my late husband's family, the Symingtons. It's much too big and ostentatious for my modest river cabin, but I keep it not only for sentimental reasons but also because I love the sonorous tone of its Big Ben chime. And I hear it now at full length because the clock is striking midnight, heralding the arrival of Christmas Day. Tomorrow is here. The hymns, sung now, are accurate. It is also much too late for a visitor.

I get up from my chair and place my tatting on a side table. I stoke the fire and let the knocker knock, hoping that he or she will become just as annoyed as I am. I go to the door. I put my hand on the knob. The knocker almost puts his fist through the door with this final, furious series of poundings. I open the door and see the last man I expect to see a few seconds after Christmas Eve, his hand drawn back as he prepares, perhaps, to knock the door down.

"Mr. Ostend," I say, quickly embarrassed that I hesitated so long to answer the door for such an important person.

"My mother sent me," he says, producing a folded sheet of stationary and almost stuffing it into my hand, as forceful with his correspondences as he is with his knocks.

I look at him, Gabriel Ostend, the river recluse. His top hat is pulled down low on the brow. The collar of his long coat is turned up to protect him from the sleet that falls harder than it fell when I walked home from church. His face is etched with a pain planted long ago. He looks like a man born a hundred years too late. I wonder why he is not in Puerto Rico like he usually is after the family's annual party in early November. I don't ask. I take the letter from him and open it. I read it. It's from Lady Ostend. I close it. I try to look Mr. Ostend in the eye, but he looks away.

"Where are we going?" I ask.

"Grindstone."

"This side or the other?"

"This side. Just upriver from McRay Point."

"You have a boat?"

"I have the *Archangel.*"

"Good. Let me get my kit." And as an afterthought, "You'd better come in from the cold."

He steps inside, just far enough to close the door behind him.

I breathe slowly as I check my bag for the necessary supplies. It's a large canvas bag, stuffed to the seams with sheets, towels, gauze packs, hemostats, forceps, a stethoscope, a blood pressure cuff, a speculum, and a DeLee suction set. I take from my office cabinet enough syringes, sutures and needles to get us through even the most difficult birth. I take from my locked medicine cabinet ampules of methergine and pitocin and bottles of lidocaine, Betadine scrub, Erithromycin and triple dye. I clearly remember sterilizing my supplies and equipment just a few days ago, but I check my notebook just to make sure I'm not confused amidst all the holiday hubbub. "22 December 1962" the entry reads. All is well.

As I put away the notebook I see the note Mr. Ostend delivered, sitting on my desk. I pick it up again and read its one simple sentence and equally simple question. The handwriting is elegant.

My Dear Mrs. Symington,
A child will be born to us this day. Would you be so kind as
to bring him into the world?
With Holiday Blessings,
Lady Ostend

"If I had time to write a reply," I say to myself, "it would certainly contain a few more questions than that."

But there is no time for either writing or philosophizing if a child is to be born. I put my kit in an outer bag, also made of canvas, as additional protection against the wet weather. I return to the foyer. I can hear the sleet tapping at the door as insistently as Mr. Ostend's knock had been. I set down my bag and put on a jumper for extra warmth and, over that, my Mackintosh. I take one final look around to make sure I haven't forgotten anything. I decide I'd better take my tatting, both to pass the time, if indeed there is time to pass, and to get closer to finishing my work for our quilt. When I turn to pick up my midwife's kit I see that Mr. Ostend already has it. He wordlessly follows me into the early morning Christmas darkness and closes the door behind him.

Mr. Henry, whose wife also attends the Methodist church and is probably home either asleep or crocheting her share of the Epiphany quilt's squares, drives us to the public dock in Gananoque. Although the river is not yet frozen and will not be for another month, a thin layer of sleet and snow coats the water like a half-cooked crust. Mr. Ostend gets out of the car and opens the door for me, again taking possession of my kit like the proper gentleman he was raised to be. The wind hits me hard as I step into the slush. We walk hurriedly to the dock.

"Be careful," Mr. Henry warns over the roar of his Buick's engine.

I look at Mr. Ostend and ask him, "Is he talking to you or me?"

"To me in getting you there. To you for once we get there," he answers.

The *Archangel* is idling at the dock. Not surprisingly, it is the only boat there. It is a large boat, at least eighty feet in length, and with its strong keel and heavy ballast it should keep us safe as we ply the stormy waters through the Admiralty Group and across the Canadian Middle Channel to Grindstone Island. It is also a comfortable boat, I find as I climb aboard, with cedar and chrome and leather everywhere. After stowing my kit in the aft cabin, which is quite warm, Mr. Ostend apologises that I should stay outside on the forward deck with him.

"Why?" I ask, preferring the warmth of the heated cabin to his silent company and wanting to centre myself before assisting with the birth.

"Safer this way," he says, and offers no further explanation.

I decide to hold my tongue and let him concentrate on piloting us away from the marina and into open water. It takes me a moment to find my sea legs amidst all the rolling and pitching. I pull my hood tight over my knit hat and stuff my gloved hands into my pockets. I close my eyes and try to concentrate on my breathing. I begin to pray the Our Father. I hear the low rumble of the engine and the ping of sleet against my Mackintosh's hood and against the boat's polished cedar. The noise prevents me from concentrating on my breathing, so I open my eyes and watch Mr. Ostend concentrate on his driving.

"Where are we?" I ask, seeing the vague outline of an island in the mist to the starboard. I also noticed that the motion of the boat has smoothed out somewhat.

"That's Forsythe Island to our right," Mr. Ostend says. "Hay Island will be coming up on our left. Hang on. Our ride is about to get rough again."

Conditions deteriorate quickly when we lose the leeward protection of Forsythe Island. The *Archangel* rolls and pitches more than it had earlier. The beam from the boat's headlight barely reaches the water. I tighten my hood and turn my face against the wind, which now drives the sleet and snow almost horizontally. The sleet and snow are also sticking to the boat, which, I recall from my husband's years on the river, causes significant changes in the boat's weight and centre of gravity, among other problems that I would rather not think about. To my relief, Mr. Ostend seems to be compensating for these dangers, as I can discern no significant change in our motion beyond what the roughness of the open water brings. He is a steady man, with the ability to keep the *Archangel* steady even in the most unforgiving conditions.

We are moving surprisingly fast through the swelling open water. I know that Mr. Ostend's intention is to keep us as far away as possible from the smaller islands and shoals that we simply cannot see. He does an admirable job of it, and in a few minutes we are making a wide turn into the Canadian Middle Channel. I feel better with the wind at our backs as we move downriver for the final leg of our journey, in part because the sleet and snow are no longer blowing into my face. Soon I can see land straight ahead of us.

Mr. Ostend glances at me and says, "There it is. McRay Point."

The sight of our destination causes my heart to race because, having been unable to centre myself, I do not feel prepared to be completely present for the mother. A calm birth is a good birth, and a midwife must remove all negative stimuli in order to create an environment where a calm birth can happen. Since knowledge also provides confidence, I decide to prepare myself in this way.

"Do you know the family?" I ask.

Mr. Ostend glances at me and turns his eyes back to the river. "Do you really want to know?"

"I should know as much as possible about the family.

Usually I would learn all I need to know at the pre-natal examinations. This situation is quite different."

We are nearing the lone dock on McRay Point now. I see a car's headlights just beyond the dock. I smile at the courtesy of people on both sides of the river who have gone out of their way to assist me on this stormy Christmas morning. At the same time, I am annoyed at having to wait for Mr. Ostend's reply.

"Who's the mother?" I ask more directly.

Mr. Ostend slows the boat for our approach. I'm grateful we're here because the wind is blowing harder and the sleet has turned to heavy snow.

"Valerie Masterson," he says.

I reflexively bring my hand to my mouth, but not before a loud, high pitched "oh!" slips out. Anyone who's been on the river long enough knows all that needs to be known about this particular branch of the Masterson family tree. Gordon, the youngest of four boys, enjoys a River Rat's luck to such a degree that he eliminated the word caution from his vocabulary. As a child he fell off his outboard motorboat and survived a hit to the head by the propeller. As a teenager he "borrowed" a small tour boat from the Canadian side and survived its sinking on a shoal in the American Narrows. As an adult he twice survived breaking through the winter ice, once on a horse, which also made it out of the water, and once on an airboat, which didn't. His fishing exploits are legendary and include wrestling a sturgeon all the way up to an island shore where the dinner he was cooking for his clients burned on the flames of the campfire. Some people say that Gordon Masterson is cursed. Others say that the river respects him so much that it refuses to take his life no matter how recklessly he tries to give it away. One thing everyone agrees on: Gordon Masterson lives on borrowed time.

Much less is known about Valerie. She stays indoors when she's not rowing her skiff on the river. She keeps to herself on the rare occasions she comes out into public. I didn't even know she was pregnant, and one way or another I usually know when any woman on the river is pregnant. Rumour has it that Valerie Masterson is half, or more, of Iroquois descent. To many that might explain the silence and the skiff. To me it matters not a bit because she, and her soon-to-be-born baby, are both children of God.

It's the depletion of Gordon's good luck I worry about. As we pull up to the dock I see that the man getting out of the car, our welcoming party, is Gordon himself.

"About time, Gabe," he says by way of greeting. "Get in. Val's not doin' so hot."

Gordon Masterson is a tall, skinny man with thin yellow hair. Haggard, I might call him if it were summer and he wore the usual undershirt and dirty cotton work trousers. But he's in an old army coat now and wears a hand-knit wool hat that has seen one too many island winters. He looks exhausted, which is not uncommon for a father-to-be. He also looks scared, an emotion he is trying to hide under his gruffness.

He smokes one cigarette after another as he drives us to his house just under a mile from the dock. I notice that his left hand, which holds the cigarette, is shaking hard and that his right hand, bone white, is clenched to the steering wheel like a vise.

I lean forward from the backseat and get a face full of cigarette smoke. "Mr. Masterson, when was the last time your wife saw a doctor?" I asked.

"Took her over to A-Bay a few weeks ago," Gordon Masterson says.

"What did the doctor say?"

"Val said he checked her out all over. She looked good, 'cept for the baby was sideways."

"Did he turn the baby around?" I ask, trying to hide my anxiety.

Gordon Masterson nods. I sit back and breathe easier

because I won't have to deal with the complication of a transverse lie—or so I think.

He takes a long drag from his cigarette, throws the butt out the window, lights another one, inhales from that and says, "Little bastard's stubborn, though." He looks at me in the mirror. "Turned right back around a few days later."

I shoot forward. "The baby turned sideways again?"

"Sure as shit. Felt it myself. His head was right up 'longside her belly."

I ask as we pull up to the family's cabin, a shack really, "Mr. Masterson, is your wife spotting blood? Is she complaining of muscle tightness? Has she had trouble sleeping?"

"Yes, yes and yes," he says as he puts the car in park. My heart races. Gordon Masterson turns around and smirks. "Know what happened the next day? The little effer turned right *back* around to where the doctor put him." He takes an extra deep puff from his cigarette. "Kid's a playful one, ain't he?"

I'm opening the door and picking up my bag, quite annoyed, when Mr. Ostend asks, "How do you know it's a boy, Gordon?"

Gordon Masterson finishes his cigarette and slips it through the window. "Had a dream," he says while looking intently across the front seat. "Saw him down there in the river, under the water, swimmin' with a sturgeon."

Gabriel Ostend is the first to notice Valerie Masterson. She stands in the doorway, one arm resting on the outer jamb, the other clutching the doorknob. She has a blanket around her shoulders that reaches down to her boots and ripples in the wind. On the snow-covered sill, back-lit by the bulb hanging from the kitchen ceiling, is the unmistakable red stain of fresh blood.

"Get her back in the house," I say without hesitation. "Carefully take her inside and lay her down."

Both men rush out of the car to help her. Her husband, in a trembling voice, yells her name as he runs to her side.

"Val, what the hell happened?" he asks.

Valerie Masterson speaks slowly and quietly. "I was lying down, waiting for you, when I cramped so badly I could barely breathe. Then the water came, with blood ..." She doesn't say anything more. She lets go of the door and allows her husband and Mr. Ostend to hold her underneath her arms. Her aura is predominantly red, grey around the belly, with hints of bright yellow around her heart and head. I look at the hem of the blanket and see that she is indeed bleeding, but not too seriously and with a good amount of water and mucous mixed in.

She says something to the two men and, to my surprise, they move her away from the house instead of back into it. Incredulous, I close the car door and rush over to them.

"Mrs. Masterson," I say as calmly as I can. "You are most likely in true labour. You must get inside."

She shakes her head insistently, although with little energy. "No," she says.

"What is this foolishness?" I ask, trying to control my temper.

"I cannot give birth here."

"And why not?"

"There's a prophecy," she says quietly.

I look at Gordon Masterson. "What is she talking about?" I ask. "What prophecy?"

He lights a cigarette and smokes it. After inhaling twice he nods his head towards Gabriel Ostend and says, "His mother. Lady Ostend. She foresaw." He smokes more of his cigarette before continuing. "Val works over there in the summers, you know, washing dishes. One day Lady Ostend calls Val into the big dining room, the one with the chandelier. Know what she tells her? She says our kid'll be born on the river and die in its waters. It's foolishness to me too, ma'am, but Val here swears by every word. What is she anyway? A hundred?"

I glance at Gabriel Ostend, who simply nods.

"Tell her the rest," Valerie Masterson says.

"Gordon?" I prompt when all he does is inhale his smoke. "What else did Lady Ostend say?"

He looked at his wife, more afraid than he had been in the car. "She says if we do this right our boy will live again."

I reach forward and brush the snow off Valerie Masterson's hair and face. She's a beautiful young woman, not much over twenty, dark-skinned and dark-haired. Her large brown eyes, quite dilated, meet mine. As we hold each other's gaze I can see her aura brighten to a beautiful red interwoven with ribbons of blue and gold light. I also notice that the wintry mix has again turned to heavy snow.

"I will tell you the truth, Mrs. Masterson," I say carefully, not wanting to upset her. "My opinion as a professional midwife is that you should birth your child safely at home. It is warm and dry in there, and we can proceed without difficulty in the comfort of your own bed." I pause to let my words take effect. "But I can also see quite clearly that you want, perhaps need, to give birth to your child on the river. I trust your intuition. I trust Lady Ostend's gift of foresight. Mr. Ostend, does the *Archangel* have a stove?"

"Yes."

"A teapot we can heat water in without it spilling?"

"Two of them."

"Then immediately upon getting to the boat, I want you, Mr. Masterson, to heat up as much water as you can. Heat it to a boil and keep it there. I also want you to wash your hands very thoroughly and refrain from smoking cigarettes once you finish that one." I look at Gabriel Ostend. "How steady can you keep your boat in this storm?"

"Not very," he says. "But I know a sheltered place, safe from wind, snow and spray."

I open the car door and motion for the men to place Valerie Masterson inside the back seat. "Take us there," I say.

A few moments later we're on the water. The western wind blows harder than it had been earlier. A veil of snow quickly hides Grindstone Island behind us, and at times hides the river below us as well. Mr. Ostend pilots the *Archangel* steadily, though, and insists he has been in much worse.

"Too fast and the frozen spray will weigh us down," he says. "Too slow and we won't be able to cut through the swell."

"How do you know where the islands are?" I look overboard and add, "how do you know where the shoals are?"

"I'm taking us upriver, into open water. Once we get to a certain point in the Canadian Middle Channel we will turn almost due north, then bear north-northeast to our destination. I am keeping us as far away as I can from the shoals." Even through the snow I can see his smile, the first one he has displayed since he knocked on my door two hours earlier. "Have you guessed our destination yet?" he asks.

"I think I have," I say. "And I find it appropriate in more ways than one."

Mr. Ostend checks his compass and nods.

I leave him to his piloting and join the Mastersons in the cabin. Valerie is asleep on the fold-out cot. Gordon is standing by the stove, watching the teapots as they approach the steaming point. The cabin is warm and is steadier than I thought it would be in the storm.

"I need to get ready," I say. "Is the water hot so we can wash up?"

"Hot enough," Gordon Masterson says. "Are you gonna see if he turned again?"

"Yes, and I'm going to see how Valerie is doing, and how close she is to giving birth. I have something for you to do. Here." I hand Gordon my notebook and a pen. "When I'm ready, turn to the first blank page, and write down what I tell you in the appropriate column."

I open a latch and let down a folding table that's hinged

to the cabin wall, noticing with appreciation that the table has a raised edge. After washing my hands and wrists, I lay my instruments and equipment out as I do at every birth: surgical scissors, needles, tweezers and gauze in the first row, syringes and injectables below them, and the larger instruments closest to me. I place my stethoscope around my neck.

I stand beside Valerie Masterson and gently remove the blankets. I lift her knees and move her legs apart, and begin to feel around her pelvis with my hands.

"The lie is longitudinal," I say. I turn to look at Gordon Masterson, who is watching me examine his wife. "You can start writing now."

"Got it," he says.

I slowly move my hands up Valerie Masterson's abdomen. "Presentation is vertex, fully flexed. Good. Head is well-engaged. I feel the neck, an arm, the bottom, the legs."

"He's all there?" Gordon Masterson asks.

"He's all there," I say.

"Turned the right way?"

"Yes. Hopefully, he'll always be this cooperative."

Gordon Masterson laughs.

I measure the heartbeat of both mother and baby and report the numbers to my scribe. I take Valerie's blood pressure and I am pleased to see that it's 130 over 85. I ask Gordon for a bowl of warm, soapy water. It spills a bit as the boat rolls over an especially large swell. As I'm washing my hands again I mention to Gordon that we must have turned north.

"Where we goin'?" he asks. "Somewhere on the mainland?"

"No," I say. "Mr. Ostend is a very wise man. Silent, but wise."

"If he was wise he'd be takin' us to the mainland."

I look him in the eye. "He's taking us to Halfmoon Bay."

"The Cathedral?" he asks.

"Yes," I say. "Not only is it a secluded place, safe from the weather, it's also a sacred place."

He hesitates and returns his gaze to the teapots. "Do you think bein' someplace sacred is what Lady Ostend meant when she told us to do it right?"

"Childbirth is always sacred," I explain, "always right, whether it happens in a hospital, in a mother's bedroom at home, or in a boat in the middle of the river. But on this day, at that place ... Mr. Masterson, I would be hard pressed to think of anything more sacred than what's about to happen."

"I'm not very good with sacred," he says. He stares at his sleeping wife. "She might be, but I'm not."

I take a few moments to recheck and rearrange my instruments, and to bond with Gordon Masterson so we can better work together to bring his child into the world. "How did the two of you meet?" I ask.

"I was fishin' in the American Channel. Val was rowin' her skiff. She saw me go overboard and offered me an oar just in time before a tanker plowed me over. I took the oar and offered her a drink when I got back to my boat. She declined the drink, but didn't decline when I asked her to marry me."

Four lives left to go, I think, but keep the thought to myself. "When was that?" I ask.

"Three years ago. And here we are, headin' off to Half-moon Bay to give birth to our son." He thinks for a moment, then breaks out in a playful smirk. "Least I don't have to worry about bein' struck down by lightening in that church," he says.

Valerie Masterson is groaning, waking up. I turn to face her.

"Valerie. We're on the river, just as you wanted. How do you feel?" I ask.

She blinks her eyes to focus them on me. "Tired. Full of energy. Calm. Anxious. I feel everything there is to feel."

"Good. I'm going to examine you now," I say quietly. "Relax. Breathe. Everything will be okay."

I wash her, then proceed with the examination, most likely the final one before she gives birth. "Mr. Masterson, write down what I say," I instruct. A moment later I tell him, "Cervix at 8 centimetres and soft. Station plus 2. Membrane is—" Just then I feel Valerie's abdominal and pelvic muscles tighten, loosen and tighten again. At the same time, she lets out a groan.

With my other hand I reach up to brush back her hair. Her eyes are open and her pupils are dilated. Her aura is still a beautiful blend of colours, dominated by red, blue and gold. "It's okay," I tell her. "Keep breathing. Breathe as deeply as you need to. Shout if you need to, or keep silent if that works best. I'm going to check your baby's heartbeat, so this will feel cold." I can hear it loud and clear at 135 beats per minute. I cover Valerie's legs. "Mr. Masterson," I say. "Wash your hands, then come here and put these on."

When he first puts on the stethoscope Gordon Masterson gives me a look of surprise, then he grins widely after registering the sound of his baby's heart. "Sacred," he says quietly as he places the earpiece on his wife's head.

I slip on my coat and hat and sneak out of the room, to give the Mastersons a moment alone and to pay Mr. Ostend a visit.

The snow is still being blown sideways by the strong western wind. The only difference now is that we're moving almost due north, causing the wind and snow to cut across the boat rather than into its prow.

He sees me out of the corner of his eye. "How is it in there?"

"So far, so good. Are we almost there?"

"I think so. Look forward and a bit to your left."

"I see land, I think."

"You see Bostwick Island. If I follow the island's shore correctly, I should be able to turn into Half Moon Bay in a few minutes."

"Do you need help with moorings?"

"I'm going to drop anchor if I can," he says. "Once we're in there, there should be enough shelter against the wind to keep us steady."

"When you have us there, will you be able to come into the cabin and assist?"

He turns towards me, startled. "Me? How?"

"I don't know yet. To keep Mr. Masterson steady enough so he can help his wife, perhaps. Or perhaps something more involved."

"I can do it," he says.

"Good. Thank you. When you enter the cabin, please wash your hands with water as hot as you can handle using the soap I left in the sink."

"I will."

"I have another question that I hesitate to ask."

"Ask it."

"A woman can become quite agitated during the birthing process. Some men find the screams quite disturbing. I thought perhaps you might find them more so."

Gabriel Ostend keeps his gaze forward and his hands steady. "I've heard many screams in my lifetime, Mrs. Symington. Most of them were screams of pain made by people on their way to death. From what I understand, and with you as the midwife, any screams I hear in that cabin will be of a very different nature."

I breathe a sigh of relief. "Yes. Thank you, Mr. Ostend."

"You'd better get back in there. I'll join you as soon as I can."

There are indeed screams when I return to the cabin. They begin as moans and crescendo up from there. I am surprised to find Gordon Masterson sitting by his wife's side, stroking her hair along her forehead.

"You're doing it right, Mr. Masterson," I say. He starts to stand up, but I gesture for him to stay where he is. "I don't need anything written down just now," I say. "It's very important that you keep doing what you're doing so your wife stays relaxed. Valerie, are you okay?" She looks at me and nods. "Good. Keep breathing. Pay attention to your body as closely as you can. When you feel your muscles contract, I want you to tighten them even more. Cooperate with what's happening. Don't try to resist. I want you to push your baby into this world. And one other thing—this might take a while."

I get my tatting and take a seat on the other side of Valerie's bed. I start humming a Christmas song again, and quickly get into an efficient rhythm of working needle and thread. Time spent sewing and waiting for true labour to begin is a deeply satisfactory time for me. It almost feels like an experience outside of time, as if the process of creation refuses to be measured by the movement of instruments made with human hands. When I do hear Valerie Masterson breathing harder and groaning, I look at my pocket watch and see that almost two hours have passed. Gordon Masterson is slumped over his wife's shoulder, asleep.

I return my tatting to its proper bag. I wash my hands again and rewash Valerie with warm, soapy water. Then I apply a coat of baby oil, lightly scented with lavender, all over her skin. I find her cervix fully dilated at 10 centimetres. At the same time, I notice the lack of movement from *Archangel.*

My activity awakens Gordon Masterson. "We there yet?" he asks.

"We are," I say.

All of a sudden Valerie screams again, louder than she had before. She convulses, too, her back arching and her bottom rising from the bed.

"Good," I say, finding a pace for my own breathing that matches hers. "Follow your body, Valerie. Nature is doing what she's always done for millions of years. Everything, all creation, is right here with you now. You're doing great. All you have to do is follow the cues. Gordon, keep stroking her hair, just like you're doing. I know this is intense. It's intense because everything that ever was, is and will be is right here right now. When you caress her like that you add something to the mixture that she can only get from you."

She lets out an especially loud shout just then and her entire body tightens, loosens and tightens again.

"Focus that energy downwards," I say. "Concentrate on pushing your energy down." I apply more oil. "Very good. You're soft down there, Valerie. Relaxed. You're doing great." I reach up and touch Gordon on the arm. "You're doing great, too. Every ounce of energy you give her flows through her and down. She couldn't be doing this without you."

"Does that mean he'll have as much of me in him as her?" he asks.

"Yes," I say, wanting to affirm his thoughts and comfort any anxieties either of them might have.

Valerie groans again and shouts even louder than before. I take a look and see the boy's head crowning. "He's moving out just fine," I say. "This little Masterson is on his way."

I also hear the door click behind me for the third or fourth time since we arrived at Half Moon Bay. I turn and give a quick nod to Gabriel Ostend as he removes his coat. He returns the nod, then moves to the sink to wash his hands. I notice that he also refills the teapot and turns the flame back up to high. After he washes his hands again, he quietly moves behind me and to my left, just out of Valerie Masterson's line of vision. Always discrete, he stands there with his head down, not looking at what he might not think proper to see.

"That's it, Valerie," I say as calmly as I can, even though

my heart is racing as fast as hers is. "His head is almost out."

Time is in flux now. Minutes seem like hours and at the same time like seconds. I check my pocket watch twice—the first time only twenty minutes have passed, the second time over an hour has gone by. As the baby's left shoulder emerges I notice that Valerie's breathing, my breathing and perhaps the men's breathing too are in synch with the rolling and pitching of the boat, which is much more soothing now than it had been outside the shelter of the bay. The shoulders come out one at a time. The torso follows, then the hips and legs. Valerie is breathing hard and pushing all the while, in perfect rhythm with the elemental force of her contractions. Slowly, I gather up the cord and straighten it to its full length. The sheets and blankets of the cot are wet with the usual amount of water and with a little more blood than usual. I look the baby over and notice that he's got a good red colour, although he's struggling a bit to breath.

"Don't be alarmed at this," I say, then give the baby a good smack on the behind. He purses his lips for a second, then cries.

"Oh!" Valerie Masterson exclaims, lifting herself up onto her elbows and seeing her son for the first time.

"You made it, Billy," Gordon Masterson says, equally in awe of the new life in his midst.

"Billy," Valerie repeats. She looks at me and smiles. "Not William, mind you, just Billy. Named after my father."

I place the crying baby on Valerie's breast so the new parents can give him all their attention. Then I move to the sink and wash my hands again, and wash Valerie again to get a better view of what I suspect is a problem that must be addressed right away.

"Valerie," I say. "You have a slight tear. When I suture it you might feel some discomfort, but not much because your body's own natural anaesthesia is still potent." I look back to Gabriel Ostend. "Sorry to say this, Mr. Ostend, but I need you now."

As he walks over to the cot, I pull the blankets up over Valerie's legs to shield his view. One by one I ask him for each instrument, antibiotic, ointment, suture and gauze pad that I need. He hands them to me quickly and efficiently without comment. When I finish with Valerie I ask him for two more blankets, which I place one below and one above Valerie's legs. Then I cover the lower blanket with a folded sheet in preparation for the placenta.

That done, I stand up and say to the men, "If you both want to take a break, now would be a good time. I need to cut the umbilical cord, take a few measurements and record some information. It's all quite tedious. Some fresh air might do you good."

Gordon Masterson stands up, and as the two men are walking towards the cabin door he asks. "Can I have a smoke now?"

"Absolutely," I say. "You've earned it."

After a few minutes of light labour Valerie Masterson passes the placenta. As she is doing so, I clean, measure and examine Billy and collect the necessary information for the doctor's and government's records. I hand her the baby and scoop the placenta into a bowl so I can inspect it. I'm just finishing up when her husband comes back into the cabin, quite animated.

"Can she stand?" he asks. "Can both of you come out here?" Then he sees the large bowl I'm holding and its dark blue and red contents. His animation turns to agitation. "Jesus!" he shouts. "What happened?" He rushes to the bed. "Val, are you okay? Is Billy okay?"

"It's Valerie's placenta," I say. "It's what's been keeping your baby alive for the past nine months. It's okay, Gordon. It's supposed to come out."

"My people bury them," Valerie says.

"One tradition here is to feed them to the river,"

Gabriel Ostend says from the doorway. Billy let's out a high-pitched grunt. "The child seems to agree," Mr. Ostend adds.

"I do too," Valerie says. "He was born on the river, after all."

Gordon Masterson looks at me. "Would puttin' the placenta in the river be more of what Lady Ostend meant by doin' it right?" he asks.

"I believe so," I say.

Valerie hands Billy to her husband, who holds his son as delicately as he'd hold a Faberge egg. Gabriel Ostend helps Valerie out of bed and covers her with another blanket, a large wool one, that hangs on a rod secured to the cabin wall. Together, the five of us go outside to the deck.

I gasp in wonder at what I see. Around us is rock, some of which is covered with a glistening coat of ice and snow. Below us is water, equally beautiful as it reflects the rock around us and the boat we are on. Above us is a blue sky on fire with the shifting reds, golds and purples of the brightening dawn. The air is calm and cold and empty of snow. The place seems as new and as fresh as the child that Gordon Masterson holds in his arms.

Valerie Masterson takes the bowl from my hands, leans over the gunwale of the *Archangel*, speaks words in what must be an Iroquois language and gently tips the bowl so that its contents slide into the water with only the slightest of splashes.

The sun is shining now. By habit my mind turns back to another favourite old hymn, which I softly hum and then sing in the crisp cold air of Christmas morning.

The Education of Lady Ostend

(March 1965)

I WRITE THIS BRIEF MEMOIR not as a key to open anyone else's door into the realm of philosophical wisdom, nor as a guidebook for any particular path on the soul's voyage towards enlightenment. For we all enter the realm of spiritual wisdom through different doors and perceive truth in different ways, and, although the destination is the same, there is more than one path we might take to get there. Nor do I presume to offer advice—my sad experience is that advice, whether solicited or unsolicited, in conformity with or contrary to the advice-seeker's plans, only strengthens the advice-seeker's resolve to proceed across whatever Rubicon he or she faces at that moment. Once the point of no return is crossed, unintended consequences usually appear that neither the advice-seeker nor the advice-giver could have predicted. Especially in the acquisition of spiritual wisdom and the practise of the subtle arts of the soul, advise is quite useless.

My underlying reason for writing this spiritual memoir is a simple one: to express my appreciation for a special place in our world, a place where I have lived for most of my life and through which I have come to know a world beyond that which can be perceived by the senses. It is a place that, as my old friend Mr. Bragdon once put it, "Has sure enchantments to release/The heart, and change its pain to peace." Bending and nearly broken under the weight of pain, approaching our own point of no return, the human race needs to know more than ever where true peace may be found.

That place is, of course, the Thousand Islands. It was here where I learned how to listen to water, rock, air and flame and how to escape the prison of time. It was here where I fell in love with Michael Dennick and where he took my name in marriage, here where we built our beloved Valhalla as a place of refuge for the world's soul-weary warriors who struggle against the perils of modern life. It was here where we raised our son and grandson and passed on to the future the good grace of the Ostend name, here where we plied the waters in the *Archangel*, that nautical messenger of light in a world of deepening shadow. It was in these Thousand Islands where I learned the immense beauty that can be found in life and—soon, very soon—in death. And here will be one of the points upon which the soul of the world pivots when a new era of spiritual harmony is spun into existence.

As a child, my travels to other lands helped sharpen my awareness of the Thousand Islands' spiritual wonders. My family visited our native village of Salmannsdorf, Austria, every year. It was there where I first identified the mysteries of the natural world deep in the Vienna Woods and upon the River Danube. In 1869, my father received the great honour of being appointed to serve under Her Majesty as a diplomatic attaché representing the newly formed Canadian Confederation. With him, my mother and I made pilgrimage to sacred sites all over the world that radiated the same divine power that I had already felt in Austria and would feel in the Thousand Islands. When I was seven years old we visited Angkor Wat. At eight I saw Mount Fuji and visited the Shinto shrines at Ise. When I was ten I accompanied my father on an expedition up Cold Mountain. In my teenage years I visited the Great Pyramid and the Sphinx, participated in the excavation of Nanna's ziggurat in Ur, prayed at the Church of the Holy Sepulchre, stood atop Mount Parnassus, where Deucalion landed his ship as the Great Flood ebbed, and danced under the full moon at Apollo's Temple on the island of Delos. On our annual trips to Austria I also visited the sacred sites of European Christendom, from Rosslyn Chapel to Mount Saint Michel, from Assisi to the Shrine of Our Lady at Lourdes.

I was nineteen when we returned to Egypt. My father was sent there to study the obelisk of Hatshepsut as a model for a Canadian obelisk, which was to be erected in Montreal on the two-hundred fiftieth anniversary of the city's founding. More personally significant, that excursion up the Nile brought to flower the spiritual senses that had been growing within me for years. For I died on that trip up the Nile, and I visited, however briefly, the realm of eternity.

It happened quite suddenly. I was standing at the railing of our bateau, gazing deeply into the depths. The reflection of the sun upon the water was a pure, deep gold. As I stared into the river I saw the ghosts of the Egyptian past skimming along its surface, keeping pace with our punt. I watched the acolytes of Isis and Osiris offer thanks for the wisdom the gods had provided. I watched the armies of Horus and Set fight their war, a struggle between good and evil that is still waged in every human soul. I saw Cheops, Chephren and Mycerinus, Thutmose, Hatshepsut and Amenhotep the Great. I saw both pharaohs named Rameses, and I saw Sety and Ahmose and queens aplenty adorned with lapis lazuli and gold. I saw ordinary men and women perform the simple yet satisfying tasks of farming, laying stone and plying their punts upon the same water which I travelled that marvellous February day.

Shadows took on substance. The ghosts of the past became visibly present. Quietly at first, then more loudly, someone whispered my name. The whispers grew more insistent, and seemed to come from all around me, and from inside my soul as well. I entered into a trance that made the

material things around me—boat, sails, people—a hazy
blur. The whisperer beckoned me to enter the river. The
water turned dark, as if the sun above were being choked
out by storm clouds, a possible but unlikely scenario. I fell
into the river willingly. The long train of ageless people
looked directly into my eyes and welcomed me into their
company.

Then Ibis-headed Thoth appeared. Awed by his presence, the figures around me became silent and bowed their
heads. The god grew in stature and radiated a golden light as
bright as the sun. He moved towards me, and I too bowed
in obeisance as his glory filled the world. He spoke in a language that I did not know, but could nevertheless
understand. He said that I was one of a select group of human beings privileged to be given the ability to cross over
into the realm of the divine. He explained that when I returned to the land of the living I would have a choice: I
could either forget this encounter and live a spiritually trun-
cated life or remember it and commit myself to the task of
honing my abilities through dedication and practise. The re-
ward for engaging in a lifetime of spiritual education? The
chance to participate in a world-changing drama that would
begin the restoration of humanity to its original, god-given
path of philosophical progress. I could not speak; I could
only see and hear. I bowed lower to signal my acceptance of
Thoth's offer of enlightenment.

The next instant my body was convulsed in pain, and a
pressure tightened around my lungs as if to extinguish my
very breath. I awoke lying on my side and expulsed two
lungfuls of water. I opened my eyes to the blazing glare of
the tropical midday sun and began to shed tears of shock.
My father and mother stood over me. Seated by my side
was Mr. Michael Dennick—at that time an associate of my
father's at the diplomatic corps and the man who had
jumped into the water and lifted me back onto the boat. My
appreciative father offered Mr. Dennick profuse expressions

of gratitude. My bewildered mother exclaimed how lucky I was that I was in the water for only half a minute, although it felt like an hour to me. Our terrified Egyptian guides refused to look at me.

I remained silent. I did not understand the full import of what had just happened to me. The experience felt like a dream until, some weeks later, I had the opportunity to reflect upon it and, several years later, had occasion to revisit the Otherworld via the magical properties of my own river. To me, that day in the Nile was a spiritual baptism into a profoundly new way of living.

That brief experience on the Nile taught me, as Thoth had said, that I was in possession of abilities that I had never before imagined. In full expectation that the world-changing drama of which Thoth spoke would soon begin, I worked to free myself from the chains of materialism that have shackled us as a civilization for over two hundred years and continue to shackle us even now. Like Michelangelo freeing a sculpture from the marble, I gradually and painfully released my soul from the layers of excess stone that covered it. The work of philosophical liberation, of exposing the true and eternal wisdom that is inside each of us, is difficult work. It is also only the first step because, after being freed, the spiritual sense must be polished to a brilliant golden shine before it is fully attuned to the beauty of the life-light that surrounds us.

The work of releasing wisdom from its materialistic constraints happens most effectively in places where the boundary between the physical world and the spiritual world is thin. I had visited many of these places as a child and would return to several of them throughout my life. As I wrote at the beginning of this essay, the most important such place in my life is the Thousand Islands of the Saint Lawrence River, where I continue to make my home.

My family owns several islands here, collectively known as the Ostend Group, located just downriver from

Grenadier Island, near Fulford Point on the Canadian mainland. As a child I acquired an intimate knowledge of our islands and their rock, of the conifers and maples that grow on their thin soil, and of the squirrels, minks, muskrats, skunks, mice, snakes, spiders and beetles that inhabit them year 'round. I still look in wonder upon the swallows, bluebirds, jays, cardinals and finches that fly and sing around me. Back in childhood, I especially adored a heron that perched on the rocks of a small weedy bay near our easternmost island. Many an evening I sat on the granite and watched her catch her food. One day she brought the fish to me and set it at my feet. The many hours I spent in the company of beast and bird may not seem like work, but it was, and I felt, day by glorious day, the liberation of my soul taking place within me.

My eyes and ears became attuned to sights and sounds that most people would not notice. The augmentation of my senses served me well when I turned my attention to the river, where the true source of the area's spiritual power lies. When I was young I sat on our islands' shores for hours. I listened to the sound of the water ebbing and flowing across the beach on one side of the islands and smashing against the granite cliffs on the other side. I saw that the unique and beautiful movement of each wave was never repeated in another. Soon I was able to move beyond my senses and perceive the deep meaning of what I saw. For example, the interplay of water and rock taught me two essential truths: that eternity and change are bound together with a golden chain forged by the gods, and that my life and the lives of all other humans are composed of equal parts of each. The regrets of the past and worries for the future began to fade into meaninglessness as my soul became aware of the dual nature of my own place in the universe.

At first, my experience of the river's magical properties happened rather willy-nilly. For instance, two years after Michael humbly took my family name, he and I watched a freighter carrying a large cargo of our hats sink off the American side of Wellesley Island. The *Oconto*, it was called, and it was already halfway under the water when we arrived. There were several marine divers working in the hull, heroically trying to salvage as much of the cargo as possible. Suddenly, the ship began to slide down the underwater slope of the shoal. All the divers made it to safety except one, Mr. Joseph Jelly, who had been deep in the cargo bay hooking up tackle to the crates. Mr. Jelly, one of the most experienced and most talented underwater adventurers on the river at the time, was in mortal danger. He had never before encountered a situation like this one. The ship was literally falling around him, and there was little chance of escape.

In a flash, a vision of what to do was revealed to me, as if I'd been told as much by the river itself. I saw Mr. Jelly holding on to his rope and air hose and manoeuvring his way through the ports and openings of the ship's interior as it fell around him. I knew that if we gave him a secure hold he would successfully execute his plan. I saw all of this in a brief instant of awareness——a moment of clarity, if you will. I directed the men to tie Mr. Jelly's rope and air hose to the railing of the barge on which we stood. A tense minute or two later Mr. Jelly emerged from the water, exhausted but very much alive. I knew my ability to see what the river showed me had helped save him. Mr. Jelly knew that his life had been spared by powers beyond his understanding. He became a close friend of ours, a dear friend who, through his own experiences on that day and others, also knew the spiritual power of our river.

Another man who understood the spiritual power of the river was Michael Dennick: diplomat, gentleman, haberdasher extraordinaire and my life-long partner in philosophical education. We had met several times when we were in our younger years. We became intimately acquainted on that remarkable trip to Karnak when I was nineteen and was granted my first vision of the world beyond. He played the hero that day, at least to those who were overly concerned about my physical safety, by diving into the Nile and hauling me back onto the boat. Soon thereafter, my father granted Michael my hand in marriage. My father probably knew that I was already very interested in this particular prospect. We were wed in 1884 in the Ostend Group. By then the stone foundation of Valhalla was already in place.

Valhalla remains a sanctuary for my family and for all those who seek a place to refresh their souls and reconnect with the all-important unseen, spiritual aspects of life. How many people have sat on its shores as the echoes of eternity and the ebb and flow of change cleansed them of the pains of the past and the cares of the present? How many people have felt their souls bore deep into the ancient rock and connect with a life-force more powerful than anything available atop the concrete sidewalks of the city? How many have sat in Valhalla's grand ballroom to watch the fires dance in the hearths and listen to the wind work its magic amongst the trees? Countless hundreds of souls have been fed here in the same way that Michael's soul and my soul are fed even to this day. There are other castles on this river. A couple of them—Boldt's and Bourne's, for example—are more grand than ours. But their spirits sleep now, abandoned by their owners and abused by their river neighbours. They might again house a family and welcome guests inside their walls, but they will never have the spiritual vitality that is built into the very core of Valhalla. Even when these stones fall, the life-giving energy of this place will continue to feed those who hunger for it.

My family celebrates its appreciation of Valhalla and the river on the first Saturday of November at the Ostend Ball. Our first soiree was held in 1886 to welcome Captain Doctor Charles Obadiah Smithson home from Egypt, where he had been serving as chief medical officer on Lord Wolseley's expedition up the Nile. The guest list that year was small, but included, in addition to Captain Smithson, the aforementioned marine diver Joseph Jelly and the American painter Frederic Remington. Their presence was significant because on that cold, November evening they confirmed something that Michael and I suspected and that Captain Smithson knew: that the spiritual properties of our Saint Lawrence River plumbed far deeper than most people outside our select company could fathom.

We were aware that the river contained some amount of a mysterious golden substance. We also knew that this substance "fed" a population of elemental beings that visited our world from the Otherworld, protected our river, and gave it much of its spiritual energy. All of us—myself, Michael, Captain Smithson, Mr. Jelly and Mr. Remington—had direct personal knowledge of both the golden substance and the elemental beings. After dinner we gathered at the main slip in Valhalla's boat house and, working together, summoned a group of undines into our presence. It was one of the most sublime moments of my life. Mr. Remington would memorialise it several years later in his exquisite portrait of me that still hangs over the main fireplace in Valhalla's ballroom.

Later that evening, Captain Smithson shared a photograph of a man he had met in Egypt and told us the man's story. The man was Naguib Malqari. As I discovered the following year when he visited the Thousand Islands, Master Malqari was, and is, an Adept, a Magus, a Genuine Master of Philosophical Knowledge and Expert Practitioner of the Subtle Arts. He influences events in ways that normal people cannot hope to comprehend. He acts in accordance with a "long view" of human history that stretches far back into the most ancient past and looks forward into the distant future. To him, our wars, our politics and the lives of our media celebrities are like shooting stars flashing across the sky for but a brief moment. His concerns, rather, are with the more stable celestial bodies that burn bright for billions of years.

Master Malqari knew of the undines' existence both here and in the Nile River. He also knew that Napoleon Bonaparte had acquired a certain amount of the golden substance in Egypt. Napoleon had exchanged some of the golden substance for supernatural aid in his war against the kings of Europe. He had also transported a quantity of it to America in advance of his own presumed exile here after his defeat at Waterloo. The gold arrived, albeit aboard a ship that wrecked in the turbulent waters upriver from Prescott. It was this gold that fed the Saint Lawrence River's undines.

I did not trust Master Malqari upon hearing Captain Smithson's story. I remained suspicious when, the following August, Michael and I met Naguib Malqari in Montreal. One of my concerns was that Malqari was associated with the Blavatsky school of Theosophy or with a group like the Order of the Golden Dawn. Another was that Malqari's intentions towards the undines were malicious. My suspicions melted away, however, when I first saw the man and felt the touch of his hand upon mine. I quickly learned that Master Malqari was no pretender. He did not acquire knowledge of the true philosophy and expertise in the subtle arts for his own gratification and enrichment or to punish his enemies. Rather, like me and those close to me, he recognised his abilities as a divine gift, and was committed to using the gift for others in their time of need. He taught me a great deal about how to hone my ability to conjure visions and how to interpret the visions when they came. He taught me how to defend myself against the threats of external malevolent forces and how to avoid the more dangerous temptations of my own ego. I learned to trust him deeply. Perhaps the greatest testament to his authenticity was his insistence that I continue to profess my suspicions of him. I did not understand why at the time, but now, after half a century of human slaughter, I understand clearly that Master Malqari did not want his spiritual powers to be manipulated by lesser men. I am eternally grateful for all he has done to show me the Way.

Naguib Malqari provided me with a foundational curriculum of readings, anchored in the world's sacred texts. In the span of a year I read the Old and New Testaments, the Koran, the Vedas and the Bhagavad Gita. I continued with the Tao-te Ching and the Analects. I read as much of the Hermetic corpus as I can find, teachings which gave me the key to unlock the true meaning of the timeless knowledge contained in the preceding books. I read as many Egyptian funerary texts and tomb writings as I could obtain, being wary all the while of materialistic mistranslations of the originals. Moving on to the Greeks, I read Hesiod, Homer and the tragedies of the fifth century. Finally, among my favourite readings to this day are Plato's dialogues, especially the *Phaedo* and books six and seven of the *Republic*. These are the foundational readings. Upon them one can build any one of several possible edifices of deep and profound knowledge. I have built several of these edifices in my time, my favourite being the one that ascended up to the towering heights of Blake's and Wordsworth's Romantic poetry.

I devoured the books that Master Malqari assigned and any other philosophical and spiritual works that my librarian and bookseller friends in Brockville could obtain. I read for hours each day, ignoring the cares of our home and needs of our son, leaving to Michael the management of our growing haberdashery. I became addicted to book learning, and I knew it. After several years of almost constant reading, I grew apprehensive that I was spending too much time filling my head with knowledge and too little time engaging with other people or contemplating the river in solitude. My anxiety manifested itself physically. I lost my ability to sleep, and thereby lost my ability to enter the dream world, where so much of spiritual reality reveals itself. I became impatient, snapping back in anger to both Michael and our son

Gabriel at the slightest provocation. I lost my appetite and my desire to share time with the birds and beasts of our islands.

My soul hit rock-bottom on a bright November day in 1893, a week or two after the Ostend Ball, when I entered an altered state of consciousness that filled me with fright. The sun was setting in the west, and I was in my skiff miles past Brockville. Whether I had rowed myself there or had coasted along the current, I did not know. I soon found myself in a different world. The Saint Lawrence moved past me in a red and emerald rush. The twilight sky above me circled around in a Van Gogh-like miasma of colour. I saw two small islands connected by a bridge. A man on the bridge was beckoning me with his arms to dock on his island and come ashore. However, the islands moved away as I moved towards them. I could barely discern shapes moving in an out of the water underneath the bridge. Occasionally, one would lash out at me as if with a serpent's tail. Yet I could not reach the island. I could not get a clear glimpse of the man. Every time I got close enough to see him and discern his face a fog settled on the water and blocked him from view. I never reached him. I lost consciousness again and woke up in my bedroom at Valhalla with Michael and Gabriel at my side. Michael said I had run aground just upriver from Prescott and had been rescued by a group of men fishing for muskie who set off before sunrise on the day after I had left the Ostend Group in my skiff. For over a year, thoughts of my downriver journey froze me with fear. I read little. I ate only what was necessary and drank only water. I even stayed in my room for the 1894 Ostend Ball, leaving Michael with the responsibility of welcoming and attending to our guests.

I found healing in July 1895 when I met Swami Vivekananda, the great Hindu mystic, who was staying in Thousand Island Park on Wellesley Island. Vivekananda taught me the simple art of meditation, which would help me effectively digest the rich food I was being served through Naguib Malqari's reading curriculum, and help me absorb the shocks of the downward journeys that my soul demanded I take. Vivekananda's key idea was unity: the unity of all religions, the unity of humanity, and the unity of creation. He said, "I do not come to convert you to a new belief. I want you to keep your own belief. I want to teach you to live the truth, to reveal the light within your own soul." I soon found tremendous joy in worshipping Isis and Jesus as two facets of the divine unity. I found myself comfortable with my entire being, the part of me that lifted me upward to the angels and the part of me that took me downward to the daimons. After meeting Vivekananda and being blessed by him, I turned to my reading with new-found vigour and, more importantly, experienced a series of spiritual encounters with the river that were deeper than any I had experienced before.

In addition, Swami Vivekananda taught me the meaning of karma yoga, the discipline of action, which was also the title of his most popular English-language book. From Vivekananda I learned that I had an obligation to use my spiritual gifts to assist those in need, to work for the well-being of others rather than for the fulfilment of my own personal goals. I applied myself to this task immediately, first by honing my skills at the various techniques I had already begun to practise. I was already quite successful at oneiromancy. Sometimes I would see visions in my own dreams; more often I would have others write down the content of their dreams and then share what I was able to discern through deep meditation. I was also quite skilled at hydromancy, which provided my vision of how to cooperate with the marine diver Mr. Jelly during the final sinking of the *Oconto*. The movement of water on the shore of the Ostend Group has placed me in an excellent natural classroom in that particular art. The same can be said for my skills at geomancy. I would often practise that craft by rowing my skiff to a secluded pink granite island, where I would meditate for hours upon the patterns that presented themselves in the shifting light and shadow. Scrying, however, was difficult for me, although I have become somewhat more effective at smoke scrying since I discovered certain herbal recipes that were favoured by the Iroquois shamans of old. While quite skilled at astrology, I hesitate to employ the art due to the prevalence of frauds and fakes among the rank and file of astrologers. Besides, to me the starry sky of a Thousand Islands night places me in the real presence of the divine. I would rather worship under the celestial canopy than interpret what I see there.

When I became confident that I could provide accurate and reliable spiritual insights to those who sought them, I began my work in earnest. I did not advertise my services. Instead, I waited for those in need to come to me. It did not take long. Unfortunately, the first person to seek me out was another Thousand Islands castle-owner, motivated by malice rather than benevolence towards his fellow man. We met at a river soiree hosted by the Emerys of Calumet. He offered to pay me a large sum of money in exchange for what he called "supernatural assistance" in bringing a rival investor to bankruptcy. The negative energy flowing from him brought a great deal of agony to my soul that evening. I understood why most people, wanting to escape the pain he inflicted by his very presence, quickly gave in to his demands. I held firm, however, and refused his request. Irate at my refusal, he threatened to ostracise me from river society. That night I had a dream-vision of the damage I could inflict on him if he followed through on his threat and if I chose the path of vengeance. My own ability to make people suffer frightened me more than the man's original threat. For several days I successfully worked to free my mind of all angry thoughts of revenge and to build a wall of protective grace around me and my family. I was not surprised when, a few years later, bad fortune fell upon the man and brought him to his knees. He died, angry and broken, just a year after that.

One river businessman I did help, and who shall not remain nameless, was Nathan Straus of Cherry Island. As you probably know, Mr. Straus was one of America's great philanthropists, his benevolence flowing out from the core of his being like a natural spring from the rock. He used the fortune he earned from his Macy's department store to do as much good as he was able. He funded schools for the underprivileged. He paid for the pasteurization of milk and distributed it to New York City's poor, thereby helping to eliminate the scourge of tuberculosis there. He gave away coal and food and provided housing for thousands of poor New Yorkers during the economic crisis of 1893. In 1897, he asked for help in his latest philanthropic project, the settlement of Jewish refugees in Israel. He knew that this Zionist enterprise was the right thing to do. He asked me to predict the possible outcomes of the project so he could follow the path that would bring the most benefit to the most people. I was more than happy to help.

I used rock from the Negev and water from the Jordan as my media. I looked deep into the future with great expectation and hope. I was shocked into despair by what I saw. There was war and destruction, fire and ash, children massacred by an enemy filled with a hatred more virulent than any I had ever known. I could not bring myself to share these visions with Mr. Straus. All I told him was that his project, whatever specific shape it took, would bring much good into the lives of many people. I encouraged him to continue his work.

But the nightmare visions would not leave me. Michael suggested that I consult Naguib Malqari for advice, which I did in a letter dated 21 October 1899. Master Malqari responded soon into the final year of the nineteenth century. Here is what he wrote:

My Dear Lady Ostend,

Your prognostication is no mistake. Ill winds begin to blow across our world. I fear the awakening of dark forces that even those much stronger than I will be unable to contain. These winds will blow strong. Some people may find shelter behind sturdy rock or under the ground and thank God for their good fortune. But they will not be safe for long, for after the winds will come the quakes, forcing those in hiding to move elsewhere. And when the ground ceases its trembling the water will flow, and finally even those who find high ground will be burned by the fire. A thousand million voices will cry out in frightened supplication. Many of them will be silenced by death.

Our world is in danger, my lady. The best you and I can do is to protect those whom we are able to protect. The enclosed charm is for you. Wear it, and continue to wear it as we enter the new century, which will be the time of wind and earthquake and flood and fire. If you wish to do so you may give it to someone you love. I put as much power into it as I was able. I am sorry that I cannot do more.

Yours in humble service,
N.M.

Enclosed with the letter was a silver chain, attached to which was a silver amulet in the shape of an ouroboros. I wore it from that day forward until I gave it to my son Gabriel on 21 September 1914, the day he disembarked for Europe as a lieutenant in the Second Brigade of the Canadian Expeditionary Force. The Ostends had been citizens of the world for a hundred years, experiencing its beauty and assisting in the alleviation of its pain. On that day of the autumnal equinox in the fourteenth year of the new century, the pain of the world came to Canada, and to my family.

I once heard a story about how the Roman Pope had a vision of God offering Satan one century, and one century only, during which the Devil's authority would hold sway over humanity. Satan chose the twentieth. The story may be apocryphal; it certainly conforms to the ominous tenor of the visions that both I and Naguib Malqari saw as the nineteenth century drew to a close. Historians have offered all sorts of theories to explain why the twentieth century is so horrid in its violence, but all of them fail to recognise the power of the elemental forces that feed on the collective malevolence of humanity. To explain the existence of so much pain and suffering in terms of economics or politics or psychology or the nebulous concept of ideology is to misdiagnose the sickness that has poisoned human civilization. Without an accurate diagnosis, a cure is impossible. I will state this fact as simply as possible: ours is a spiritual disease.

As I read the news stories coming from across the ocean—stories of the earth-shaking artillery at Verdun, the thick mud of Flanders Fields, the flame-throwing monstrosities of Hooge and the mustard gas poison of Loos—I recalled Master Malqari's warnings that earth, water, fire and air would become combatants in this new age of mass death. The violent, subconscious power that had been burrowing its way upward for decades was now an obvious fact. The Great War proved that many men of high standing tried to harness that dangerous power for their own ends.

With the help of Master Malqari's amulet, Gabriel lived. He survived the battles of Vimy Ridge, Second Ypres, Passchendaele, Amiens, Cambrai and, in the last days of the war, Mons. The story of his survival and heroism is his. I will only mention that when he disembarked at Prescott in January 1919 he showed me the amulet that still hung around his neck. It had saved his life from artillery barrages and machine gun attacks on more than one occasion.

Gabriel was paraded down the streets of Prescott, Brockville and Kingston as a national hero. His friends in Ottawa tried to convince him to run for public office. The amulet had protected him, but it did not save him.

Psychologically and spiritually, he was a broken man. Michael and I both encouraged him to stay at Valhalla to recouperate, which he still does, fifty years after going off to war. Gabriel spends most of his days fishing from his skiff or piloting the *Archangel* up and down the river. A generous man, he opens Valhalla to a dozen of his wartime friends for the week of the Ostend Ball. After the ball he relocates to San Juan, Puerto Rico, where our family owns a second hat factory.

After the Great War, and despite the false evidence offered by materialists that physical well-being and the comforts of life are the best measures of human progress, the spiritual condition of humanity continued to erode. More and more people, it seemed, welcomed the power of destruction into their lives. Death came from all directions as the century wore on. The mechanised brutality of the *Blitzkrieg* and the new weapons that pulled from the atom a power beyond even what the greatest pyromancer could imagine are only two examples. Most horrifically, the Nazi's systematic near-destruction of Europe's Jews brought to reality the nightmare vision that I dared not communicate to Mr. Straus. It grieves me to the core of my being that my people, the Austrians, bear much responsibility for this greatest of all atrocities. The Second World War was death-obsession taken to an extreme conclusion. We remain enslaved to that obsession. The only change in the two decades since then is a new subtlety in how governments advertise and sell death to the public.

Meanwhile, men who think they are gods have tried with equal energy to suppress the elemental forces of the world. They think they have tamed the atom. They believe they have successfully harnessed the power of wind and water. Here in the Thousand Islands, the rock has been dredged and the river dammed, and men in Ottawa and Washington nod in satisfaction that the Saint Lawrence has surrendered itself to their control. One of my most recent visions tells me otherwise—it shows a time to come when the river and rock will endeavour to restore the harmony of life that has become unbalanced by mankind's hubris. I do not know when it will happen. I do not know exactly how it will happen. I do know that Valhalla will be one place where the restoration of harmony will begin. I also know, as I was told by Thoth on that day in the Nile, that I, or my progeny, will play a significant role in the unfolding drama of world renewal.

For almost a century these islands on this magnificent river have been my home. Now, as my time in this world nears its end, I begin my final task, which is to prepare Valhalla for its purpose in the life-struggle to come. The sum-total of my life's education has been this one conclusion: that the Thousand Islands is a place of life from which a deeper and more advanced state of human knowledge and sympathy will emerge. Soon I will pass the stewardship of our castle and its destiny to my grandson Raphael. It will be his responsibility to watch and wait. If the appointed time arrives during his lifetime, it will be his duty to set in motion a plan that I will complete before I die. If his life ends before the appointed time arrives, he will pass the responsibility to watch, wait and act to a future generation of Ostends. I have prepared the ground and sowed the seeds. It is for someone else to reap the harvest.

Billy Masterson Finds His Way Home

(July 1886; May 1942; July 1977; August 2002)

BILLY MASTERSON SWAM. He stayed to the starboard side of the *Oconto*, just swimming, trying not to think because thinking hurt. In fact, everything about him hurt. The arms he no longer had felt dislocated, the legs that were no longer there felt broken in a dozen places, the lungs he no longer used for breathing felt punctured by non-existent ribs.

"Pain is just nerve endin's shootin' information to the brain," he mused. "So how's it workin' now? Do I still have nerves? Do I really need a body to feel pain? If I had a head would I have a concussion?" And the question that kept coming back: "What the eff just happened to me?" Thinking about pain sent new and worse waves of it coursing through his being. So Billy shut off his mind and swam.

He would eventually understand that what he felt was deeper than pain, more severe than the ache of bone or the throb of muscle. What he felt was a spiritual anguish, like when you lose someone you love or when something you yearn for is just out of reach, in the firm grasp of someone you despise. On that summer day in 1886, having been shot back through time by a force he did not yet comprehend, the ghost of Billy Masterson experienced suffering at its most profound level.

"I've been double dipped," he thought, the idea sneaking into the corner of his consciousness. "First I lost my life, now I've lost my present circumstances." It took him only a moment to make his decision. "I'm gonna find my way home," he said, moving faster to catch up to the bow of the *Oconto*, knowing exactly where to go and what to do. "I'm gonna find my way home and get some vengeance on those effers who did this to me."

It was a century earlier than when he was used to, but it was the same river, and Billy knew it better than he knew anything else in the world. He swam beside the *Oconto*. He considered what he saw and what was not yet there to see. He marveled at the freshness of the water, not yet spoiled by oil spills, discarded plastic bottles, jet ski fuel and island sewage. He looked with astonishment at the number and variety of fish swimming around him, both with and against the current. He came to a full stop and almost got run over by the *Oconto* when he saw the most astonishing fish of all: a twelve foot long sturgeon coasting along below him. The fish's scales and barbs shone like spiked armor as it method-ically worked its snout along the muddy river floor, feeding on bottom dwelling crustaceans that tried in vain to hide from the beast that preyed upon them. Billy slowly descen-ded to about five feet above the fish.

When it had eaten its fill, the sturgeon rolled halfway, flipped its winged tail, and rose up to Billy's level. Was it reaching its pectoral fin out to him? Billy moved closer. The fish turned its head slightly and mimicked his motion. Billy moved downward and back up, as he had while playing por-poise on this same section of the river before he was cast back in time. The sturgeon mimicked him again. "This might get interesting," Billy thought, feeling better about his situation and feeling renewed by the company of his new friend. He sped up and slowed down. He stopped and dropped to the river floor. He touched the bottom and sped back upwards to the water's surface. He caught up to the *Oconto* and swam laps around the boat. He dipped under its hull and turned his ovals into figure-eights. The sturgeon moved with him all the while, never falling behind and never missing a single dip, rise, stop or turn. The games were fun, but soon Billy's thoughts turned elsewhere.

Where on the river were they? The channel and the smaller islands along it didn't look the same as they would in Billy's own time because they had not yet been blasted and dredged to create the Saint Lawrence Seaway. What he saw to his starboard must be Wellesley Island, but, again, the underwater geography was difficult to interpret because of water conditions that Billy wasn't used to. Had the gold given him the ability to escape the water? He believed it had, based on the fact of his forced flight that got him here in the first place. If possible, he would take a look at his surroundings from the air.

Billy said goodbye to the sturgeon. "Keep your ears open, big guy. Or antenna, receiver ... whatever you have. I might need you someday. If I do, I'll be givin' you a call."

The fish seemed to hear him and understand because it blinked and swished its tail before it descended under the *Oconto* and disappeared into the channel. Billy watched it go, hoping they would meet again.

Billy said "up, up, up" until he was moving at a forty-five degree angle towards the river's surface. He was still worried about not being able to ascend out of the water. When he emerged into the air he was flying alongside the hull of the ship. His mind gave a shout—"Eff yeah!"—and he did a few horizontal loops around the freighter to celebrate. He stayed low in case human eyes could see him. His first instinct was to look up and find the bridge.

"Idiot," he told himself when he saw nothing above but stars in the sky. "The bridge won't be here for another fifty years."

He therefore had to go by what he knew of the landscape. He saw cliffs alternating with smooth shorelines and weed-filled bays. There being no permanent cottages yet on this section of Wellesley Island, there were no lights on the shore. That in itself was a clue—he was past Westminster

Park and not quite to the Peel Dock. His intuition of looking up to the bridge wasn't that far off the mark because he
was near the spot where the bridge would eventually be
built. Then he saw Brown Bay. For confirmation of his location he plunged back into the water and moved underneath
the *Oconto* and emerged on the other side. He recognized
Swan Bay, on the mainland, at once.

"So we're about four miles from my new friends' cave,"
Billy thought as he returned to the water. "That means
we're also about four miles from where this ship goes
down." He remembered that no one was injured in the
wreck, which soothed his growing anxiety because he also
felt that his foreknowledge of events gave him a responsibility to forestall any suffering that events might bring. "An
old school river shipwreck," he said to himself. "Should be
quite a show."

He descended to about ten feet below the surface and
raced ahead to the Granite State Shoal, where he stopped
and waited for the wreck to happen. Holding steady against
the current at about three feet deep, he saw the *Oconto* approach and figuratively held his breath.

The ship headed straight for the rock. There had to be
some sort of navigational error involved, some misreading
of the charts, because the ship didn't veer an inch or slow
down even a fraction of a knot. It was full-steam ahead for
its ill-fated encounter with unmovable rock. Its bow passed
the shoal unscathed, but just barely. Its stern hit the granite
with a thud and a crack. Nails popped out of their boards.
The boards themselves bent and snapped and collapsed
against the unyielding granite. The tar caulking along the
seams unraveled like a ribbon in the wind. The ship
stopped. Air bubbled out of the rips in the starboard hull.
Water churned as the stern began to fall. The *Oconto's* wood
moaned and continued to crack as it moved against the
granite. Water gushed into the hole as air kept billowing out
of it. Finally, the aft hull of the ship came to rest at a

substantial angle about seventy feet deep. Billy moved closer, wanting to take a look at the damage and to trace the line where the bow of the boat emerged from the water.

As he was doing so he heard the now-familiar hum of the undines behind him. Reassuringly, it sounded like only two "voices" above the low register descant. To be sure, Billy said "I hope you're the good guys" before he turned around.

"We are your friends," the undines said.

Billy turned to face them and saw an image taking shape above them. It was a woman, a beautiful woman, standing behind the railing of a boat or barge, looking down into the water with a concentrated look on her face. Her blond hair was tied back. He face was without makeup. Billy recognized her immediately from a painting he'd seen over a dozen times.

"Why are you showin' me Lady Ostend?" he asked.

"She will be here soon," they replied.

"Her hats are on this boat," Billy said, recalling what Lady Ostend's grandson, Raphael, had told him about the wreck of the *Oconto*.

"They are. More importantly, she needs to be here to help rescue a diver who will be trapped in the sinking hull of the boat. You need to help as well."

"Why?"

"The diver is of great importance to the well-being of the river. He must not perish. Not here. Not now."

Billy thought for a moment. "Do I get anything in return?"

"What do you want?" they asked.

"I want to go home," Billy said, trying not to sound pleading.

"It shall be done," they replied right away.

Billy considered this. "So if I help her save this diver, she'll help me get home?"

"We will."

"Why not help her yourself then help me?"

"We can only perform certain tasks. We can cause you to move through time, as you already discovered in quite unfortunate circumstances when you encountered our cousins. We can also heal. We cannot, however, cause material substances to move. We can neither hold the *Oconto* steady as the diver escapes, nor guide the diver through the wreckage. You, however, can do either, if you so choose."

Billy thought back to the wonderfully energizing charge he had received from the Darlingside source of Napoleon's gold. "Touchin' stuff's one of my new powers, huh?"

"One of them."

"What else can I do?"

"Your senses of hearing and sight are more acute than you might yet realize. As you know, you have the ability to leave the water and proceed through the air. You also have the ability to travel through time on your own, but you will need to experience the sensation a few times and become familiar with it's consequences before you can begin to control it. We will assist you in that."

"A few times? What will you do, send me back to my present then bring me back here then send me back to the future again?"

"No. Once you help Lady Ostend free Mr. Jelly from the sinking hull of the *Oconto*, we will send you forward in time gradually through a series of intermediate stops. We have tasks for you to accomplish at each stop. You will know what they are when you arrive. We also promise you that you will end up in 2001, or soon thereafter."

"Sounds like a good deal," Billy said.

"A once in an after-lifetime opportunity," the undines said.

"Was that a joke?"

"A what?"

"Never mind." Billy laughed anyway. "So what do I do? Hang around here and wait for Lady Ostend to show up?

Or are you goin' to boot me into the future like your cous-ins did?"

"She will be here soon," they repeated. "Until then, you can do anything you like. We will find you and alert you when it is time to return."

So Billy cruised the river, both below the surface and above it. He investigated the grandiose Frontenac Hotel on Round Island, crossed the river to Wellesley Island and toured Thousand Island Park. He studied the mechanics of a steamboat as it disembarked from its Clayton dock. Pre-dictably, he spent most of his time swimming with the fish, because it was this activity that gave him strength and moved him further along the road to healing. Feeling good, he returned to a few of the sources to see if their effect was cumulative or just a one shot deal. He felt tingles, like being recharged he guessed. He was back at the source in the Ad-miralty Group when the friendly undines appeared.

"We must return," they said.

"Already?"

"You have not yet gotten used to this new experience of time," they explained. "Three minutes, three hours, three days, three weeks, three years—all of these distinctions you once used to make are quite irrelevant now."

Billy considered this for a moment. "Then how can I make sense of things?" he asked.

"This is one river we are in. This is one world, one uni-verse, one great living soul in which we live and to which we are connected. In the soul of the world, everything is and al-ways remains both here and now."

"Then why all the talk before about shootin' me through time and the discomfort I'll experience when it happens?"

"Because there are very powerful external forces that act upon both space and time. All of creation, but especially hu-mans, have free choice, and the choices made by created beings that have not yet entered the realm of eternity are what create time itself, at least as you used to understand it."

Billy moved around the three undines and positioned himself squarely in the flow of the gold.

"What are you doing?" they asked.

"I'm hopin' the Forsyth Island source gives me some brains to figure out what the hell you're talkin' about."

"Shall we put it more simply?"

"Please."

"Roll with the changes," they said. "Outside of eternity, the only thing that is truly real is change. Changes are all around you, in the air, in the water and even in the rock. Roll with the changes."

Billy felt like he was smiling and nodding his head. "Roll with the changes," he said. "That's somethin' I can do. That's somethin' I've always done. Now let's go save ourselves a diver."

Back at the wreck, Billy positioned himself under the *Oconto's* ripped hull. He reached out and actually touched a splintered piece of wood jutting out from the gash. His new skin felt like jelly with the wood pressing up against it. Billy wondered if his new skin might burst if he pressed any harder. He pulled away because he didn't really want to find out.

He heard a voice in his mind, hushed but insistent. "Help me," the voice said. "Help me see where he is and what he is doing." Billy guessed correctly that the voice was Lady Ostend's. "I see you," she said. Billy looked up and was surprised to see her, too. The *Oconto* and everything in it had become transparent—everything, that is, except for the marine diver, who Billy saw in the foreground, about forty feet above him. The scene reminded Billy of Wonder Woman's airplane from the Justice League comic book he used to read—would read—as a kid.

Billy locked eyes with Lady Ostend. "Tie the rope and his air hose to the barge railing," he said. "I'll make sure he holds on tight. I'll guide him through the cargo bay and through the trapdoor on deck. Hurry. His life depends on you."

A moment later the *Oconto* started to sink. Billy quickly moved through the gash in the hull and up to the diver's position. "His name is Mr. Joseph Jelly," Lady Ostend told him. Billy nodded.

Billy gently wrapped the rope and hose around Joseph Jelly's torso just underneath his shoulders. He tied them together and handed them to the diver, who seemed not at all surprised at what was happening. Mr. Jelly took hold of the rope and hose with a firm grip and gave them a tug. They were secure.

The ship scraped and moaned as it fell. It accelerated as its weight shifted off the rock. Billy held Joseph Jelly around the waist as water whooshed around them. He concentrated on guiding the diver left and right, forward and back, as the ship descended. He still saw through the entire ship and could see the holes in the various decks as they approached. There were six total through which they had to pass. This was not a difficult task. Billy wondered if all of them on his journey home would be this easy.

The diver was through the fourth hole when Billy scraped against a board with several nails protruding from it and got the answer to his earlier question about the durability of his new skin. He was pleased to see that his skin did not puncture, but rather became more viscous and slid over and around the nails and board, despite their obvious sharpness.

"We're almost there," Mr. Jelly said as they moved cleanly through the fifth aperture. The diver looked over his shoulder and gave Billy a smile.

"You can see me?" Billy asked.

"You look like one of those water things," Joseph Jelly said, "only more like a human than a fish. What's your name?"

The question gave Billy pause. He knew from watching movies and reading novels that blending the past and present could have serious repercussions. Granted, telling the diver his name wasn't quite the same as murdering his own grandfather, but Billy still hesitated. "It's just my name," he finally told himself. "It can't amount to that big of a paradox."

"Billy Masterson," he finally said. "Born, raised and died on the river." He kept quiet about when.

"Well thank you very much, Billy Masterson," Joseph Jelly said as the sixth and final hole, the trap door out to the deck, passed around them. "If you had a hand I'd offer you mine to shake." He nodded upwards. "You'd better let go. Except for Lady Ostend, I don't think the others would be as comfortable with your presence as I am."

Billy saw that they were approaching the surface and let go of Mr. Jelly's waist. He turned and moved down along the Granite State Shoal, watching the *Oconto* fall into its permanent grave. "Keep on divin'," he said to Mr. Jelly as a farewell.

IN AN INSTANT Billy felt himself transported through space and time again, although not nearly as harshly as he had been the first time. He knew exactly where he was when he landed, even though he was dizzy and a bit nauseous. All of it was there, just like he was used to: the fireplace and the portrait above it, the massive oak table polished to a reflective sheen, the chandelier with its one hundred and two crystal lights. He was in the corner of Valhalla's grand dining room. He quickly slipped behind an upholstered armchair when he heard voices approaching from the east corridor.

"These accusations are absurd," a woman said. He knew it was Lady Ostend before she walked into the room.

She wore a simple dark blue dress without the adornment of jewelry. Her loose hair fell over her shoulders. The man who followed her was in a blue military uniform. His hair was cut short and barely protruded from underneath a beret. Lady Ostend stopped walking, turned around, cocked her hip and placed a hand on the back of the chair at the head of the table. With her other hand she pointed a finger at the uniformed man. "I have been a loyal citizen of the Dominion and subject of the Crown since I was born, as were my parents and their parents, dating back to the reign of George the Third."

"Do you still visit Austria?"

"Not *now!*" She loaded the second word with contempt, although without raising her voice.

The officer made a mark on his clipboard. "When was the last time you visited Austria?"

"In 1936. And I was deeply troubled by what I saw there."

"Are you in contact with any other Austrians, Germans or other subjects of the Third Reich currently residing in Canada?" When it was clear that Lady Ostend would offer only a glare in reply, the officer turned to another page and placed the clipboard and a pen on the table. "We will need their names," he said.

She tapped the back of the chair and sighed. "I understand that you're only doing your job, Colonel Perriman. I understand the condition of heightened anxiety that exists now that the war has come to Canada." Lady Ostend glanced at the clipboard and pushed it aside. "But I will not help a scared and confused government impinge upon the freedom and dignity of those I love."

"The question is, Mrs. Ostend, how did you *know* that the war had come to Canada?"

"Pardon me?"

"You contacted your friend Lieutenant Smithson three days before the *Nicoya* was sunk and four days before anyone in the government knew there were submarines in the Saint Lawrence."

Lady Ostend held her patience, but just barely. Billy, watching from behind the green chair in the corner, was engrossed.

"Do you know me, Colonel Perriman? Do you know who I am? What I do?"

"You are quite famous, Mrs. Ostend."

"Then why do you ask me how and where and from whom I obtained my knowledge?"

Billy watched Colonel Perriman's confidence slip away now that he was being asked the questions. Perriman glanced at his clipboard, back up to Lady Ostend, and then to a point somewhere near the floor. "I ... I don't believe in magic," he said.

"Magic is a cheap card trick," Lady Ostend said dismissively.

"I don't believe in the supernatural," the Colonel tried.

"Tell me, Colonel, does the Canadian government take seriously Adolph Hitler's belief in the supernatural? Does the Canadian government understand the essence of his obsessive pursuit of otherworldly power? If not, it had better start, because *that's* why Hitler's U-boats are here." She let go of the chair, picked up the clipboard and pen and held them out towards the Colonel. "Take your clipboard back to your superiors, Colonel. And tell them to think twice before sending you back her for another interrogation." She returned her hand to the chair and tipped it backwards a bit. "In fact, tell your superiors that if one of them would like to visit Valhalla, he can sit in the same chair in which my dear friend William Lyon McKenzie King sits for dinner and, after that, remain seated for his annual divination."

Colonel Perriman blushed at the mention of the Prime Minister. He followed Lady Ostend to the door, trying to save face by apologizing for just following orders. The butler was waiting in the hallway to escort Colonel Perriman to the front door. Lady Ostend returned to the dining room, closed the door and locked it. She inhaled deeply and sighed, then walked over to the corner of the room where Billy was hiding.

"You can come out now," she said.

That surprised Billy. She could see him? He obediently came out from behind the chair and couldn't help feeling as embarrassed as Colonel Perriman had.

"Can you hear me?" he thought. "Can you understand what I'm sayin'?"

"Yes, I can hear you. I heard you that day at the *Oconto*, too. I knew you'd come back, but I didn't think it would take this long." Billy was watching her mouth as she spoke. Oddly, he heard her words a half-second before her lips moved. "I know you don't hear me as a person with ears would hear," she said, "but I prefer to talk anyway because, in situations like these, talking helps keep me grounded."

Lady Ostend moved back to the table and sat down in the chair where Mackenzie King annually sits. "What did you think of our colonel?"

"Quite the pri—" Billy stopped himself. "Arrogant windbag," he said.

"Sadly, he probably *was* just following orders," Lady Ostend said. "If his superiors are as narrow-minded as he is, we don't have a chance in this war. Billy, do you know why you're here?"

"I know where I am. I sort of know when I am. Beyond that, I'm pretty much clueless."

"Allow me to provide some context. Today is Sunday, May 17, 1942. Last week, a Canadian ship was destroyed by a torpedo shot from a German submarine. This happened in the Gulf of Saint Lawrence. Our government seems to believe that the sole German objective is to sink merchant ships bound for England. I know differently. I know that the Nazis also seek to locate and acquire a supply of Napoleon's gold, and to use it in their effort to conquer the world and destroy civilization."

Billy was uneasy. "Like the colonel said, how do you know?"

Lady Ostend looked right at him, causing Billy to wonder how much of him she actually saw. "Do you know Naguib Malqari?" she asked.

Billy thought it over. "I will in about sixty years," he said honestly.

"Good. Master Malqari visited me seven years ago and warned me of the true nature of the Nazi threat. He assured me that, of all the dangers to face humanity up to this point in our history, none was more dangerous than the Third German Reich."

Billy shivered. Back in his old life, he loved watching cable TV shows with footage from World War II. He loved watching the German tanks roll through Poland and the Stukas scream over the horizon, and especially loved seeing the crisp leather coats that the officers wore. Now that he was in the midst of the war, he didn't feel so glib about how he used to yell "kill Commies!" at the television screen.

"Our friends in the cave on the other side of Wellesley Island informed me that German submarines are in our river," Lady Ostend said.

"The same ones who sent me here," Billy asked.

Lady Ostend nodded. "Back to my original question, then. Do you know why they sent you here?"

"They said I'd have a task to accomplish."

"Do you know what that task is?"

"After hearin' all this, I think I can offer a pretty good guess."

Lady Ostend stood up and went to a window that offered a wide view of the river and of the Canadian mainland beyond. "We're in a bind, Billy. We cannot destroy the gold because the river needs it. We cannot draw a net across the river at Prescott and Ogdensburg like you Americans once drew a chain across the Hudson at West Point. The military will not listen to us. Prime Minister King will listen

—has listened—but he knows, quite correctly, that to broadcast the true aim of the German U-boat offensive in the Saint Lawrence would be to commit political suicide." She returned her gaze to Billy, who was next to the table, just six feet away. "Do you have any ideas about how we might get ourselves out of this bind?"

Billy thought back to what he knew about the river before it was dredged into the seaway. "Can U-boats get through the rapids?" he asked.

"The undines tell me they can."

"So basically, short of blowing them up, which would scare the pants off the government and just about everyone else in Canada and in the U.S., there's not much we can do to stop them."

"Correct."

"Then we hide the gold," Billy said, thinking back to what he knew and thinking forward to what he would someday learn. "We conceal all six sources with rock and mud and whatever else we can find. We keep the Nazis from findin' it. We keep anyone from findin' it until after we win the war."

"Six sources," Lady Ostend repeated. "Master Malqari suspected that the gold associated with Napoleon was not the only gold in our river."

"He was, is and will be right about that," Billy said.

"If we hide it," Lady Ostend asked, "will someone, someday, be able to find it again?"

Billy thought about Charlie and Mary Flanagan and the River Rat Reporters. He thought about everything he would go through in his personal quest to find the gold. "Yes," he said, cautious not to give too much away. "Our river is changin'. Some of the changes are bad, others are good."

"Do you mean the seaway?" Lady Ostend asked, taking Billy by surprise. She noticed this and continued. "The Saint Lawrence Seaway has been a project in men's dreams for many years. I quite expect that one day it will be built."

"Do you know what other changes are comin'?" Billy asked.

"I have seen glimpses of the future," she explained. "Master Malqari has too, and we have discussed our visions at length. We see people, many people and all the destruction they bring when they gather in large groups. We see oil and sewage in the water. We see fish dying from the pollution and from human predation. But we also see people who care about this river more than they care about anything else in the world. We see them working to clean the river. We see them fighting to save the river and planning how to protect it."

"How's the gold fit in?" Billy asked.

Lady Ostend smiled. "The gold seems to have a certain ability to conceal its intentions," she said. "Neither myself nor Master Malqari can quite discern the place of the gold in what we see of days to come. Perhaps you will have a hand in that."

"Malqari told me ... will tell me that the gold is runnin' out all over the world." Billy paused because the feeling in his heart told him he was crying, although he knew he had no tear ducts and thus no tears. Moreover, Billy knew he was crying about something that was to happen in the future rather than something that had happened in the past.

"Billy?" Lady Ostend gently said.

"That's why I'll do it, Lady. About seventy years from now. That's why I'll jump into the river to free Malqari's ship so the next threat to the gold can be stopped."

Lady Ostend moved over to where Billy was standing and reached out her hand. Somehow, Billy felt her touching his brow and his cheek, wiping away the invisible tears, salving the pain.

She spoke softly, this time not moving her lips at all. "The river loves you, Billy Masterson. Always remember that the river loves you as if you were one of its own."

BILLY, WITH QUITE A LOT OF HELP, did hide the gold. The help came first from the undines, who agreed to place themselves in and around all six of the gold's sources and enchant the gold so that no one, especially the Germans, could see it. Then Billy got help from his new sturgeon friend, who called upon twenty-seven of his sturgeon friends to assist him in moving sand, mud and rock over each source's opening. Finally, Lady Ostend called upon the assistance of the river itself. Using wave and current and other forces beyond the comprehension of man and ghost alike, the Saint Lawrence moved rock and shifted its floor to seal off all but the slightest trickle of gold.

One Nazi submarine did find it's way upriver, although it never did find the gold. Billy remembered that he would learn about the U-boat later in life, about how it was dive-bombed by planes from the Canadian Air Force and sunk near French Creek in Clayton. In fact, Billy, like many other River Rats, would someday see with his own eyes the anchor marked with a Nazi swastika that remains on display at a local marina. The anchor would be the sole evidence of a little known episode in river history.

"This subterfuge will not last," the undines said to Billy and Lady Ostend when the work was completed.

"Yet it may last long enough," Lady Ostend said.

Billy, back in the water, looked from one undine to the next, all the way around the circle. "Task accomplished?" he asked.

They answered with their humming, then with a flash of light that sent Billy again reeling through time. He and Lady Ostend were looking at each other as it happened. Billy thought he would never see her again.

THIS TIME THINGS WERE MORE FAMILIAR. The water of the Saint Lawrence was murky, and Billy, even in his disembodied state, felt its greasy stickiness. There were boats everywhere—loud ones, dirty ones, mostly cheap fiberglass ones that leaked gas and oil and whose owners tossed candy wrappers and glass soda bottles freely into the water. Billy poked up out of the river and almost got run over (if it were possible) by a speedboat cruising way too fast in what looked to be a no-wake zone. Shirtless men with more hair on their heads and bodies than Billy had seen on a man in years were in the boat. Lynyrd Skynyrd's "Freebird" blared from the boat's speakers. He looked around and saw the windowless husk of Boldt Castle, marked with spray-paint graffiti from top to bottom.

"Must be the seventies," Billy thought.

The question was, of course, what was he doing here? Was his task to check on the status of the coverings that hid the gold? To move those coverings away and reveal the gold? To tell someone, Ben Fries perhaps, the gold's where-abouts?

Billy went back under water and submerged into the depth of the channel, where the water was quieter and cleaner. He was confident that, once again, the river itself would lead him in the right direction. After coasting with the current for a time Billy heard the now-familiar humming all around him. He was certain these were his friends. He stopped and treaded water.

"Time travel's gotten easier," he said. "This jump only left me with a headache."

"You should now be able to travel through time without our help," they said.

"Don't I have something to do?" Billy asked.

"Yes. Your final task is a simple one. There is a girl who needs to learn that the river is special. To use a terrestrial metaphor, she needs a seed planted in her soul, a seed that will germinate and grow in due time and flower at the prop-er time. You must plant this seed."

"You guys can't?"

"We are too different. You are still very much human. Some humans, children especially but also adults whose spiritual senses have not been dulled, can see and hear you. The girl will listen. In her heart, she will remember."

"What's her name?"

"You will know her as Mindy McDonnell."

Another surprise. "Where can I find her?"

"She is nearby. The river will take you to her."

"What do I tell her?"

"Words of encouragement. Words she will remember."

"Guess I'll figure something out," Billy said.

"We're confident you will," they said.

"After that I'm done?"

"After this simple task is accomplished you may go home."

"How? You said I can do it myself, but how?"

"It will be easier than you think. You might not even notice right away how your surroundings have changed. As we said once before, roll with the changes and all shall be well."

"I want to get revenge on those creatures who sent me back in time," Billy said.

The undines became agitated, swishing back and forth as if they were in pain.

"What?" Billy asked.

"You cannot undo what has already been done. You cannot change what cannot be changed. They could only do what they did. There was no other way."

"No other way? What they did hurt like hell! Back in the day I'd smack—" The undines swam back and forth now. Billy interpreted the movement as a collective shake of the head and cut the thought short. "So there's nothing I can do about them?"

"Not for some time, and under very different circumstances."

"Will you smack them around for me?"

"No."

Billy paused, allowed himself a moment to calm down. "So this is goodbye?"

"This is goodbye for now," they said. "Be at peace and roll with the changes. All shall be well." With these words they disappeared by slowing their vibration and blending into the water.

Billy went on his way in search of the young Mindy Mc-Donnell, wanting even more to be home. He found her easily enough. He knew she'd be on vacation, so he went from one state park to another looking for her. She wasn't at Keewaydin or Goose Point. There was no one at Mary Island. He found her at Wellesley Island State Park, probably the most obvious place of them all. It was nearing dusk, approaching Billy's favorite time of day on the river. He found her playing in the water with a doll. He floated on a wave a few feet away from her. As far as he could tell, Mindy was not aware of his presence.

She was sad. Her mother was calling her from the shore, telling her it was time to come in. Billy thought about how, almost twenty five years from now, he would dance with this young girl as a woman in Raphael Ostend's ballroom and dance with her again on the *Archangel's* deck.

"I don't want to go," she said glumly. "I want to stay here forever. I don't want to go."

Billy thought she was talking to him. He dipped deeper into the water and rose back up when he figured that this moment was as opportune as any he would get.

"I don't want you to go, either," Billy thought.

Mindy clutched her doll closer and scanned the water around her. She waded towards Billy. He thought she was going to step on him. He moved away from shore. "I don't want you to go, either," he said again. He also figured he'd better keep it simple so as not to confuse her too much when she tried to wrap her mind around what was happening.

Mindy stopped. She searched the water again and then

focused on the spot where Billy tried to hide. She didn't say a word. She just looked into the water and smiled. When her mother called her again, she dutifully waded onto the shore.

Billy never saw her again—that is, would not see her again until she came to Jimmy's with Tom Flanagan in November 2001 on the night before Billy's last Ostend Ball. Had he gotten through? He thought so. He saw the smile on her face when she looked at him. He guessed that the six-year old Mindy McDonnell would carry the experience for the rest of her life, even if it was buried deep in her memory. He hoped, as the undines had said, that the seed he planted would someday come to flower.

BILLY MOVED BACK into deeper water and went upriver. He rounded Wellesley Island and moved through the Narrows. He didn't stop at the cave or anywhere else near Thousand Island Park. He stayed in the channel and high-tailed it up to the bridge. Just past the bridge he caught sight of a shadow above him. He ascended out of the water and saw the *Argoma*, a laker that was often seen plying the seaway's waters between Montreal and various Great Lakes ports. Billy slowed and settled onto the ship's wake. Riding the wake had been one of his favorite river activities when he was flesh and blood. He wanted to know if it still held the same thrill now that he had changed.

After a few minutes he realized he was no longer alone. There was someone in a boat on the other side of the ship, riding the port-side wake.

"It can't be!" Billy shouted in his mind. "Holy effin' hell, it is! Andrew Hibbard!" Billy concentrated hard and repeated Andrew's name.

Andrew glanced his way then stood motionless and stared. He impressively kept his flat-bottomed boat directly centered on the wake as he looked in Billy's direction. Billy was definitely back in his own present circumstances, as he liked to say. He knew this because it was in the summer of 2001, last summer, that he had helped Andrew shop for the new fishing boat.

Suddenly, with Billy riding the wake and Andrew watching Billy ride the wake, Billy had a clear and jarring vision of things to come, almost as if he were again transported into the future, if only for a few seconds. He saw the river under attack. He saw upheavals around him that seemed impossible, even in his new state of being. He saw loved ones under threat. He saw Andrew Hibbard himself in grave danger as Andrew put himself at risk to save someone that Billy could not identify. The vision faded. Billy turned and saw Andrew still looking his way.

"I've got to tell him," Billy said to himself. "I've got to tell him something." So he concentrated on Andrew's name, repeating it over and over again. But what should he say? Would Andrew really believe him if he told him what he saw? Billy decided to keep it simple, as he had with Mindy. He offered advice instead of prophecy.

"Keep ridin' the wake," he thought, directing the words over to Andrew. "A big change is comin', but you'll be okay if you keep ridin' the wake."

Once he said the words, Billy felt a great sense of relief. As he fell back into the water, immersed again in the loving goodness of what he knew was the crystal river of life, Billy also felt that his new present circumstances were the best he could possibly ask for.

Finally, and for the first time since before he was able to remember, Billy Masterson was home.

Also by Thomas Pullyblank

Available from Square Circle Press
www.SquareCirclePress.com